MURDERS of HERKIMER COUNTY

THIS BOOK CONTAINS

AN ACCURATE ACCOUNT

OF THE

Capital Crimes Committed is the County of
Herkimer,

FROM THE YEAR 1783 UP TO THE PRESENT
TIME.

AMONG THOSE OF RECENT DATE ARE

The Wishart Murder, the Druse Butchery,
and The Middleville Tragedy

THE FACTS WERE GATHERED FROM THE OFFICIAL
RECORDS

OF HERKIMER COUNTY, AND OTHER RELIABLE
SOURCES,

BY THE AUTHOR,

W. H. Tippetts

Entered according to Act of Congress, in the year 1885 by W.
H. TIPPETTS, in the Office of the Librarian of Congress, at
Washington.

Wilderness Hill Books Edition 2008

ISBN # 978-0-6152-1955-4

Cover design:

Front cover depicts Roxalana Druse awaiting execution at the Herkimer County Jail. Back cover depicts Roxalana on the witness stand.

Images are from engravings in *An Innocent Woman Hanged; Mrs. Druse's Case*, Old Franklin Publishing House, 1887

Editor's Introduction

In 1884 and 1885 Herkimer County was in a state of turmoil as first one, and then three more murders excited the attention of the public. In May 1884 the battered body of John Wishart was found in a ditch near Frankfort. Within days his son-in-law was indicted for the murder while Wishart's daughter and wife were charged as accomplices. In November of that same year the body of Charles Derby was recovered from the Erie Canal. His body showed eividence of foul play but his killer remained unknown. Two months later, the suspicions of neighbors in the town of Warren uncovered a murder that had occurred in the previous month.

Roxalana Druse, her daughter and nephew were charged with the murder of Mrs. Druse' husband William. What was particularly horrifying about this murder was not only that his own family had allegedly killed a husband and father but that his body had been dismembered and burned in an attempt to conceal the crime. Barely a month later word came from Middleville that a respected physician, Dr. Moritz R. Richter, had shot to death Professor S. Clark Smith of Fairfield in a dispute over the property of the physician's wife.

In this heightened climate, W.H. Tippetts set out to write a history of capital crimes in the county, going all the way back to 1783. Drawing on county records and interviewing coroners and attorneys, Tippett evidently rushed his work into print before the year 1885 was over, and well before Roxy Druse was convicted and sentenced to hang at a trial which attracted statewide and national attention.

The resulting book, which has been preserved in only a few copies, exhibits all the prejudices and haste of its author. In fact, those very prejudices are what the make his book such an interesting window into the thinking of

Tippetts' and earlier generations. During the first decades of the 19th century juries tended to return acquittals and judges tended to impose notably short sentences when a homicide occurred in the context of "a fair fight" between two adult males. Homicide of those perceived as outsiders, including Indians and "a Jew pedlar" led to swift acquittals in the early history of the county.

Crimes that caused public revulsion, however, met with stronger penalties, as in the instance of ten year old John Bowman who was sentenced to death in 1811 for the murder of a girl his own age.

Of Tippetts' himself, I can learn little. Susan Perkins, executive director of the Herkimer County Historical Society reports that the 1880 Census states that "he was then about 28 years old, born in New York State, and was a traveling journalist. In that year he was living Rochester, NY. with his mother and grandparents.

This book is exactly the same as Tippetts wrote it, with the exception of chapter arrangement. I have grouped together his short notes on capital crimes from the earlier history of the county, and placed a piece of literature, entitled "Dialogue of the Skulls" and reportedly penned by an anonymous juror, at the back of the book. I have also added a Table of Contents although the chapter titles are Tippetts' own.

Table of Contents

TO THE PUBLIC.

In presenting this little work to the people of Herkimer County, the author desires to make a few explanatory remarks.

The record of murders as published in the following pages, is as near as possible, correct. Owing to the destruction of the Clerk's office by fire in 1804, when all county records were destroyed, it becomes impossible to give any accurate account of the capital crimes committed before that date. Since the year 1804, and in the earlier portions of the century, the Oyer and Terminer court minutes, and the hundreds of criminal indictments filed in the County Clerk's office, are our only source of record. These have been carefully scanned and each point fully established before publishing. I have endeavored to be accurate in regard to data, and have confined myself wholly to facts.

The details of many of the earlier crimes, are lost in the misty obscurity of frontier history. The only one of which I find any record is the supposed murder of an Indian, by that old revolutionary veteran, John Adam Hartman, in the year 1783 or '84. From that time until 1805 no record exists, and even in the succeeding years, the records are meager in regard to details. Before proceeding farther, the reader will pardon me for giving a few historical points in regard to the old county of Herkimer.

Herkimer county was formed from Montgomery February 16,1791. The name, according to an old authority, was originally Erghemar, and was variously written for many years. Onondaga county was taken from it March 5th, 1791, and Hamilton March 16th, 1798. The north line was completed by the formation of St. Lawrence March 3rd, 1802, and the present outline fixed on April 7th, 1817. The county contains 1, 745 square miles, and is considered to be the fifth in point of size in the State. Herkimer county is one of the most picturesque counties in New York, and contains within its borders a large tract of the famous hunting grounds of the North Woods.

The county was first settled by the Palatinates from Germany, in the year 1722. During the " French and Indian " war of 1756-7, the Palatine village--now Herkimer--was twice destroyed by the Indians, and many of the settlers killed. In the years immediately following, and during the stormy days of the revolution, murders and massacres were of frequent occurrence, and life held of but little value down to the years bordering on the present century.

Herkimer county, today, ranks among the foremost counties of the State, in wealth, culture, industries, and, as this book testifies, capital crimes. Although a number have been sentenced to swing, the records of Herkimer would seem to prove that no one has as yet undergone the extreme penalty of the law. From reliable sources that cannot be gainsaid, I am furnished with information that leads me to discredit the old saying "That no murderer was ever hung in Herkimer county." The statements are, in a measure, traditional, but to my judgment they bear the insignia of truth.

During the present century, however, the sheriff has never been called upon to exercise his chief functions. In view of the fact that nine persons are now awaiting the convening of the next " Oyer and Terminer court" in this county, and that they are all, either charged with murder or as accessories, I will not argue the question whether or not an execution would prove conducive to a better state of affairs. This book is not published for the purpose of molding public opinion--that to my mind is already formed,--but for the sole purpose of placing before the public a complete and accurate account of the many different murders that have taken place in this county.

Before bidding you farewell, I would state that in my search for information, I have met with nothing but the most courteous treatment from our present county officials, and also many others approached upon the subject.

My acknowledgments are due to County Clerk Palmer M. Wood, Special Deputy, A. T. Smith, District Attorney A. B. Steele, Sheriff Brown, the Hon. Samuel Earl, Judge T. C. Murray, Col. J. A. Suiter, Coroner Nellis, and the proprietors of the Herkimer Democrat and Ilion Citizen, for the use of their files for reference.

Hoping that this little work may be kindly received by the public, I remain, yours faithfully,

W. H. TIPPETTS.

John Adam Hartman and the Indian, 1783

John Adam Hartman was one of the earliest settlers in the county of Herkimer, and was known throughout the surrounding section as a hunter and scout of no mean ability. He was born in Edenkoben, Germany, and emigrated to this country before the outbreak of the revolutionary war. The War of Independence found him a firm partizan of the colonies, and he served throughout the seven years of its duration with credit to himself and terror to his enemies.

Soon after the peace of 1783, Hartman fell in company with an Indian, at a tavern in the west portion of what is now known as the town of Herkimer. The fire water of that day was of a potent nature, and as the son of the woods imbibed the fluid lightning, his tongue became loosened, and be commenced to boast of exploits and murders committed during the past war. To his inebriate mind no braver Indian ever wore a moccasin. He was a Big Chief, and would brook no contradiction. Hartman listened to all this with apparent good will and continued to ply the red man with whiskey.

The Indian finally became somewhat excited, and in a spirit of bravado, produced a tobacco pouch as a trophy. The article was made of the skin taken from a white child's arm, and tanned or dressed with the fingers, nails and thumb still attached. Hartman's blood boiled, and he became fired with a resolution that, drunk or sober, that Indian should not boast of his evil deeds much longer. He inquired which way he was going, and stated that their road lay together. They left the hotel in company, and took a path leading through a swamp towards Schuyler.

As Hartman was unarmed, and the Indian carried a heavy pack, besides his weapons, he offered to carry the red man's rifle. The Indian willingly embraced Hartman's offer and they disappeared in the underbrush bordering on the swamp.

The Indian was never seen again alive.

When Hartman was asked, shortly afterwards as to his whereabouts, he replied: " that the last he saw of him he was standing on a log in the swamp, and suddenly fell off as though he was hurt. About one year afterwards the body was found near a log, embedded in the morass, and near by, his rifle, pack and other weapons forced down in the mire, showing conclusively that plunder was not the object of the murder. Hartman was arrested and tried at Johnstown, the then county seat of Tryon county, and acquitted.

In after years during conversation relative to the affair he would distinctly and minutely describe the tobacco pouch, and indulge in sundry hints in regard to the Indian's very mysterious death. Hartman survived the Revolution more than fifty-three years and finally died at Herkimer April 6th, 1836, aged 92 years and 7 months. He is buried in the cemetery attached to the Dutch Reformed church, on Main Street, in the same village, where his head stone may yet be seen by the curious.

This murder, if murder it can be called, may be classed among justifiable homicides, as the red devil richly merited the fate fortune bestowed upon him.

A Legendary Murder

The story of the following murder is wholly traditional, but according to the best authorities, explicit reliance may be placed upon the statement. The woman's name is unknown. but the facts as gathered by the writer are substantially as follows:

Between the years 1791 and 1798, a woman was tried in this county for the murder of her husband, and sentenced to death. The sentence of the court was carried out, and the murderess duly executed according to law.

After the execution a number of medical students obtained possession of the body, and during the succeeding night carried it to a small island in the West Canada creek. Previous to this a large cauldron, or kettle, had been taken to the island. This was filled with water, a fire started underneath, and as soon as the water reached a boiling temperature pieces of the body thrown therein. The students kept the fire burning until the flesh was completely separated from the bones. These were carefully fished out of the "devil's broth," cleaned, polished and the skeleton put together.

Old citizens state that the skeleton remained in possession of the students for many years, but was finally broken up and destroyed.

Acquittals and Short Sentences

Previous, to the year 1805--as before stated--no authentic record of trials for murder exist. The County Clerk's office was totally destroyed by fire in 1804, and, as far as known, all county papers and books destroyed also. In consequence of the primitive methods en vogue during the earlier portion of the present century, the criminal history of Herkimer county is hard to trace. The Oyer and Terminer court minutes, with a few scattered indictments. are our only sources of information. The court minutes of 1805 give us the first recorded murder trial.

-W.H.T.

Rufus D. Stevens, 1805

On Wednesday, June 19th, 1805, Rufus D. Stevens, a resident of this county, was tried at an Oyer and Terminer court for the crime of manslaughter. Chief Justice Kent presided, with Nathan Willlams as District Attorney. The jury found the prisoner not guilty of the crime.

Nicholas Hiltz, 1807

The next case that appears on record is that of Nicholas Hiltz, who was tried for the crime of manslaughter on Wednesday, June 24th, 1807, before Chief Justice Van Ness, Nathan Williams, District Attorney. The prisoner pleaded not guilty, a verdict of the same being returned by the jury.

Aaron R. Clark, 1809

The first conviction occurred June 6th, 1811. On Wednesday, May 31st, 1809, Aaron R. Clark was indicted for murder, and brought before Justice

Yates, Nathan Williams, district attorney. The case was continued until the next term of court, the prisoner in the mean time, being let out on bail of $1,000. At the next term, Clark could not be found, but was finally secured, and the case came up for trial June 6, 1811. He was convicted of manslaughter, and sentenced to State prison for three years and three months. The prison of the State was then located in or near New York City, and all criminals sentenced in the State were accordingly taken to the Metropolis for confinement.

Joseph Lincoln, William Ayers, and John Wood, 1811

On June 5th 1811, before Justice Van Ness, Nathan Williams, district attorney, Joseph Lincoln, William Ayers and John Wood were tried for manslaughter and acquitted. The court discharged the jury without their returning a verdict.

Samuel Bennett and Peter Johnson, 1822

The case of Samuel Bennet and Peter Johnson came up for trial before Chief Justice Platt, on December 22d, 1822, with Simeon Ford as district attorney. Bennet pleaded not guilty of murder or manslaughter, as charged, and the case went to a trial. Michael Hoffman and James McCauley were the attorneys for the defendants and did their best to secure an acquittal. The court adjourned until December 12th, when Bennet was found guilty of manslaughter and sentenced to State prison for ten years. Peter Johnson was discharged. No record of the crime can be found.

Sanford Klock, 1835

Sanford Klock, of Little Falls, was tried June 3d, 1835, before Justice Nathan Williams, James B. Hunt, district attorney, for the killing of Richard Williams. Klock was indicted for striking Williams upon the head with a club, from the effects of which he died on April 10th. The prisoner pled not guilty and was so acquitted by the jury.

Jared Webster, 1835

Jared Webster, of the town of Danube, was indicted on September 17th, 1835, for the murder of William Bellinger, on August 10th, same year. The prisoner struck Bellinger on the right side of the head with a stone, killing him almost instantly. The trial came off on March 16th and 17th of the following year. The jury, after due deliberation, gave in a verdict of acquittal. Judge Nathan Williams was the presiding justice, and James B. Hunt district attorney.

Abram J. Casler, 1847

Abram J. Casler, of the town of Manheim, was tried June 10th, 1847, before Justice Mason, George B. Judd district attorney, for the murder of William Knox, April 12th, the same year. The jury convicted him of the crime of manslaughter.

John Andersen, 1849

On October 2d, 1849, before Justice Mason, Geo. B. Judd, district attorney, John Anderson was tried for manslaughter. The indictment charged him with the killing of Daniel Cooley, in the town of Schuyler, August 26th, 1849, with a club. He was convicted, and sentenced to Auburn prison for the term of 3 years.

John Allen, 1850

John Allen, of the town of Schuyler, was indicted for murder on April 1st, 1850. Allen was accused of killing a Jew pedler on or about February 23d, in the same year. The case came up for trial before Judge Philo Gridley,

Geo. B. Judd district attorney, on September 4th, 1850. The trial created considerable excitement and over forty witnesses were examined. After a long session, the court directed the jury to return a verdict of acquittal. The Hon. Samuel Earl, Hon. Robert Earl and Volney Owen appeared as counsel for the defense, and it is owing to their untiring efforts that the prisoner was discharged. Allen had formerly been a soldier in the English army, and when the verdict was given a tall rough looking individual seated in the back portion of the court room sprang to his feet, and cheered enthusiastically for the prisoner. There was no question but what Allen was innocent of the crime charged

John Bowman, a Boy Ten Years of Age, Tried for Murder and Sentenced to Death, 1812

September 14th, 1812, John Bowman, a lad of about ten years of age was tried for murder, found guilty and sentenced to be hung on the fourth day of December. The boy was ably defended by Daniel Cady, Esq., one of the best lawyers and jurists in the circuit. Nathan Williams was district attorney and conducted the case for the people.

At that period the pardoning power was vested in the Legislature, instead of the chief executive of the State, as at present. The counsel for the defense, Mr. Cady, seconded by other able lawyers, succeeded in securing the passage of an act on November 10th, 1812, commuting Bowman's sentence to imprisonment for life.

The crime for which the boy was tried and found guilty, was the killing of a playmate, a little girl of about his own age. He struck her on the head several times with a club, and then dragged the body into the Mohawk river, afterwards covering it with brush.

Bowman, before his trial, was confined in the old county jail, and one day, to the great surprise of the jailer and sheriff, he turned up missing. A search was instituted, but Bowman was nowhere to be found. In the course of a few hours, however, he nonchalantly entered the front door, and when questioned about his absence, replied, "that he was tired of the jail and simply went out to take a walk."

Bowman, when the crime was committed, was between nine and ten years of age, and at the time of his sentence could not have been much over ten.

He was taken from Herkimer to New York city to serve out his sentence. The Hon. Samuel Earl informed the writer that he has made every effort to gain a knowledge of Bowman's fate, but was only able to learn that he was an inmate of the prison on Blackwell's island as late as 1820. Since that date nothing is known of his whereabouts.

The Brutal Murder of His Wife
by Samuel Perry, 1826
His Trial, Conviction and Sentence
The Murderer Commits Suicide
His Body Stolen by Medical Students

Along in the summer of 1826 the people of Herkimer county were horrified to hear of the brutal murder of Lydia Perry, by her husband, Samuel Perry. The facts of the murder show it to be a cold blooded and heartless affair.

Samuel Perry was a resident of the town of Newport, and on the day of June 1st, 1826, came into the house with a medium sized butcher knife concealed in his right coat sleeve. His wife, Lydia Perry, was at the time of his entrance standing at the ironing table, ironing, with her back to the door. The murderer came up behind and put his arm around her waist, pretending that he was about to kiss her. With a quick motion he drew the knife from his sleeve, and cut the miserable woman's throat. Mrs. Perry dropped to the floor and died almost instantly. It is claimed that Perry then
stabbed himself twice in the breast, with the same knife, but as the blade encountered a rib each time, the wounds given were not of a dangerous character.

Perry was arrested and taken to the old jail, in Herkimer, at that time standing where the new Court House is now located. He was indicted for murder on September 11, 1826, and pleaded not guilty. His trial was postponed until Wednesday, December 13th. The case was called the next day before
Judge Nathan Williams, with George H. Feeter as district attorney. Michael Hoffman, Lauren Ford and O. G. Otis appeared as counsel for the criminal. For the three days during which the trial lasted, the little village of Herkimer was thronged with people. Over forty witnesses were examined and the case created so much

excitement that many drove from other counties to attend court.

On the 16th day of December the jury found Perry guilty of murder in the first degree. On prayer of his counsel a respite of judgment was granted by the court, to enable the prisoner to remove the indictment and proceeding to the supreme court, to obtain their decision on certain exceptions, taken in course of trial, to the opinions and decisions of this court in empanneling the jury. A new trial was not granted, however, and the criminal was sentenced to be hung,.

During Perry's incarceration in the jail, under the care of Ira Crane, jailer, he adopted the modern dodge of insanity. He became so violent that the jailer had him chained to the floor, but the situation becoming uncomfortable, Perry became more tractable, and was finally removed to another cell. The question of Perry's sanity became a theme for discussion and it was finally decided to take him to Albany and have his case subjected to a rigid examination.

John Dygert, the Sheriff, was about to start with the prisoner for Albany, and was walking toward the jail for the purpose of bringing him out, when James Byers, a friend of Perry's, notified him that the criminal had committed suicide.

Col. J. A. Suiter, a well known resident of Herkimer, and a boy at the time of which I write, was playing near the jail and heard Byers' exclamation. Our knowledge of what follows is taken from Mr. Suiter's statement, as he entered the jail and was present when Perry died.

When Perry's cell was entered he was found on his knees beside the bed, covered with blood. In his throat was a ghastly wound, stretching nearly from ear to ear. It was evident at a glance that the wound was mortal. He was taken from the floor and placed upon the bed. The prisoner expressed a wish for a glass of water, which was at once brought; he drained the contents, but as the organs of the throat were severed the fluid rushed forth from the wound. The sight was a horrible one; the crimson life blood flowed faster and faster, and the wretched man, as he felt the pangs of dissolution rapidly approaching, thrashed from side to side, scattering the blood over everything that was near. Perry was a stoutly built man with a bull neck, and he died very hard.

Immediately after his death a search was made for the knife. As Perry had already attempted suicide, the attaches of the jail were careful not to leave a knife or fork in his cell. Near the center of the floor stood a pail of water, and as the water was colored with blood, it was evident to all that the suicide had committed the act over the pail. When the pail was emptied a razor was thrown out with the water. An examination of the blade showed that the prisoner had thoroughly made up his mind to commit suicide, as the edge of the razor was dented and nicked where it had come in contact with the back bone, or spine.

Dr. Ethridge, a medical student, who happened to be present, sewed up the wound in Perry's throat and the body was made ready for burial. Some little difficulty was experienced in obtaining a permit to bury Perry in the cemetery back of the present Methodist church, but the matter was finally arranged, and he was buried after dark in one corner of the grounds. At that time Herkimer county did not boast of a hearse, and the persons who had the funeral in charge were at a loss to find a conveyance for the coffin.

Just before dark two men drove into the town with a rickety old wagon and a spavined horse. They were both somewhat intoxicated, and when asked for the loan of the horse and wagon, exclaimed; "Holy horrors, no! We'd be spooked for the rest of our lives."
Their natural fondness for whiskey soon led them to forget all exterior circumstances. A few choice spirits gathered around, plied them with liquor, and both father and son, for such was the relationship they bore to each other, quickly sank into a state of oblivion, as complete as though they had passed the river Styx. The wagon and

horse were appropriated, the body taken to the grave, and all that was left of the murderer and suicide deposited in its last resting place.

It had become generally known that a party of Fairfield medical students were desirous of obtaining the body, hence a watch was kept up at the grave for four or five nights succeeding the funeral. On the fourth night two tramps called upon the watch, and being provided with drugged whiskey, proceeded to dose the four or five who were guarding the remains. When they awoke from a prolonged slumber the tramps had disappeared, and with them the body of Samuel Perry.

The Murder of the Indian, Peter Waters, by Nathaniel Foster in the North Woods, 1834

The Foster murder case, as it is termed, has proved a fruitful source of conversation ever since the trial. As it is often quoted and freely discussed by many who have no perfect knowledge of the facts, I have taken pains to obtain a true statement of the murder, from the most reliable sources.

Nathaniel Foster and Peter Waters, a Saint Regis Indian, were both hunters and trappers in the northern portions of the county. They had long traversed the trackless waters and forests together, and were apparently the very best of friends. Sometime during the year or summer of 1834 Foster and the Indian were stopping at a tavern in the northern portion of the county. As the old saying has it, "when the whiskey is in, the wit is out," they both fell to quarrelling about some trivial affair. Foster was a man of some sixty years of age, and when intoxicated, often proved quarrelsome. The Indian was in the prime of life, and, like the most of his race, never forgot a kindness or failed to revenge an injury:

Foster abused Waters shamefully, threatening to give him a whipping, and calling him all the various names of the wilderness that he could lay his tongue to. War was imminent between the two, but they were finally separated and the Indian persuaded to leave. Just before departure he uttered a threat in Fosters presence, saying that he would have his life in revenge for the insults heaped up on him. Foster heard this, and at once made up his mind to assassinate the Indian. Without saying a word to any one, he obtained a knowledge of the Indian's course and made preparations for waylaying him. Waters left the tavern in company with two white men, embarked in a canoe on the river and set out for a trip through the Fulton chain of Lakes. Foster, by a short cut through the forest, came out on a point some five miles in advance of the party, and took up a position in the underbrush. The scene chosen for the crime was a picturesque one. The little point of land was located on one side of the channel, connecting the first and second lakes, and but a few rods from the clear expanse of second lake.

Foster waited patiently until the canoe arrived opposite his lurking place, when he leveled his rifle, and shot Waters through the heart. He was shortly afterward arrested, brought to Herkimer, for trial, and indicted that same year.

The murderer was ably defended by the following named lawyers: Joshua Spencer, Aaron Hackley, G. H. Fester, Lauren Ford; and Elisha P. Hurlburt, afterwards Judge of the Court of Appeals, and the only one of the number now living. The Hon. Hiram Denio was the presiding judge and James B. Hunt, district attorney, who conducted the case for the people, assisted by Simeon Ford, Esq.

The trial was an interesting one, and during its continuance created considerable excitement. A singular feature of the trial was the overruling of the Circuit judge by the three side judges. A plea of justifiable homicide was advanced by the defense, the claim being made that an Indian's threats, by reason of his nature and savage education, were to be considered more dangerous than those of a white man, and that Foster, in slaughtering Waters, had merely acted in self defense. The jury before whom the case was tried were principally of German descent, and as stories of Indian massacres were still prevalent in the county, they evidently considered the killing of Waters as of little moment, and apparently acquitted the prisoner on the grounds of justifiable homicide.

Cold Tea, as a Deadly Agent, 1849

Mrs. Daniel S. Neeley, of Fairfield,
Poisoned by her Son-in-law, R. E. Dickey.
The Murderer Commits Suicide

On the 13th day of May, 1849, the people of Fairfield were horrified by the murder of Mrs. David S. Neeley, wife of David Neeley, by her son-in-law, Dr. R. E. Dickey. At the inquest, held by Coroner Putnam, the following facts were elicited:

R. E. Dickey was a son-in-law of the deceased, having married a daughter of Mrs. Neeley's. The union did not prove a pleasant one, and after a short season of domestic infelicity, the wife returned to the home of her parents. It was the custom of the household to use cold tea as a beverage throughout the day and, on the morning of the murder, the teapot was as usual set aside for this purpose.

A short time after breakfast Nancy Neeley drank a small quantity of the tea, and was taken deathly ill. She recovered after an interval and at once proceeded to clean the teapot, throwing the contents into a pail and scalding the utensil thoroughly. She then made another pot full and placed it upon the table. During the forenoon Mrs. Neeley drank of the contents and at once went into onvulsions. Her condition rapidly grew worse, and the unfortunate woman died within the hour.

During the excitement Dickey, who was stopping at the house at the time, emptied the contents or the teapot out of the window, and was afterwards observed cleaning the porch floor. Suspicion at once pointed to him as the probable murderer, and a warrant being issued, he was arrested, just as he was about to board the train at Little Falls. Coroner Putnam at once impanneled a jury, and ordered a post mortem examination made as to the cause of death. The testimony of the physicians conducting the examination, proved that Mrs. Neeley came to her death by a dose of Prussic acid, and

Dickey was accordingly held for the Grand Jury.

While the inquest was in progress the prisoner succeeded in making his escape, and for a time baffled every effort made by his pursuers. He was followed so closely, however, that he at last took refuge under the floor of the wood house attached to the residence of a relative. The whole neighborhood turned out in pursuit, and Dickey was finally run to earth.

When the murderer learned that his place of concealment was discovered, he opened a small pen knife and cut his throat. He lived but ten minutes after being drawn from his hiding place.

The Luther Fratricide Case, 1856

The Luther murder occupied the attention of the public during the year 1856. Thomas Luther, the murderer, killed his brother, in the town of Norway, with an ax. The brother was a married man, and both Thomas and himself were somewhat addicted to drinking. One evening while the brothers were together, the bottle flowing freely, a quarrel arose between them. From words they proceeded to blows, and Thomas Luther perceiving an ax, seized it and struck his brother a fatal blow in the neck. He continued to ply the ax, until he had completely severed the head from the body.

The case was tried before Judge William J. Bacon, Volney Owen, district attorney, on September 9th and 10th. The prisoner plead not guilty, but the jury convicted him of murder in the first degree, and he was sentenced to be hung on the 28th day of October.

Judge Graves interested himself in the fate of the criminal, and finally succeeded in securing from the Governor, Myron H. Clark, a commutation of the sentence to imprisonment for life. Luther remained in prison for eight or ten years, a pardon being finally secured for him through the intercession of Judge Graves.

Cold-Blooded Case of Poisoning, 1861
Miles Wilcox Poisons His Friend, Geo. G. Platt

   Miles Wilcox was indicted for murder on April 23rd, 1861. He plead not guilty, and the case was set down for trial on October 28th, before Circuit Judge Joseph Mullin, with S. S. Morgan as district attorney. Wilcox was charged with the murder of George G. Platt, in the town of Litchfield, on August 23rd, 1860. He was a married man, and for some reason or other, suspected that his wife and Platt were altogether too intimate. On the 23rd of August, at a picnic, Wilcox produced two bottles of whisky, and invited Platt to drink. In one of the bottles he had previously placed a quantity of strychnine, and from this bottle poured out a drink and handed it to Platt, drinking himself from the other. Platt died soon after in great agony.
   Wilcox was arrested and tried for the crime--as already stated--on October 28th, 1861. Roscoe Conkling defended the prisoner, and made an eloquent plea in his behalf. Wilcox at first entered a plea of not guilty, but was finally allowed to withdraw that, and plead guilty of manslaughter in the 3rd degree. Judge Mullin protested against accepting the plea, but was overruled by Judge Graves, County Judge, and the Justices of Sessions. Judge Mullin stated that he did not wish to go on record as accepting a plea of manslaughter, when the evidence produced in open court tended to prove the criminal guilty of a deliberate and cold-blooded murder. The plea was, however, accepted, and the prisoner sentenced to Auburn for two years and six months. Wilcox died in prison before the expiration of his term.

Daniel Walrath Kills his Wife and Daughter, and Then Commits Suicide, 1865

During the last of November, 1865, the community of Little Falls was terribly shocked to learn that Daniel Walrath, of that place, had killed his wife and daughter, and then committed suicide by shooting himself.

Mr. Walrath was about sixty years of age, and at the time of the murder, was undoubtedly suffering from a temporary aberration of mind. His wife, Paulina, was about fifty years of age, and his daughter, Mary Josephine, about ten years old. Mr. Walrath bore the reputation of being a good husband and a loving father. He was comparatively well off, but for some little time previous to the dreadful act, was noticed to be in a despondent mood, and expressed himself, on several occasions, as in fear of want. By continually brooding upon the subject, his mind at last gave way, and without warning to the unfortunate victims, his insanity culminated in their deaths, and his own, by his own hand. It is supposed that the crime was committed on Monday morning, November 26th.

The next day and the day following, the house was noticed to be closed, and as none of the family were seen about, an investigation was made. Mr. Van Valkenburg entered an upper window by means of a ladder, and on coming down stairs saw the bodies of Mrs. Walrath and her daughter in their night clothes, both dead, with their throats cut. He thereupon gave the alarm; it was first supposed that burglars had committed the deed, but the finding of the body of Mr. Walrath in the wood house chamber settled the manner of the crime beyond a doubt. He had knocked his wife and daughter down with a heavy cane, which was found, and then cut their throats with a razor, then with bloody hands he deliberately loaded his gun and went into the wood house chamber, to which he was tracked by bloody footprints, and by means of a cord attached to the trigger of his gun, he shot himself in the head.

The coroner impanneled a jury, who after hearing the testimony decided that the wife and daughter came to their deaths from the hands of Mr. Walrath, while suffering from a fit of temporary insanity. Mrs. Walrath was a sister of the well known lion tamer, Herr Driesbeck, who on one occasion, while passing through the village of Little Falls, gave a private exhibition of his power over the brutes, especially for his sister's benefit.

The writer is indebted to counsel for Judge Jacob H. Weber for the particulars of this affair, and also one or two others, which I take this occasion of acknowledging.

Murder of a Hotel Landlord
at Frankfort Hill, 1866

On Monday, May 7th, 1866, five indictments for murder were presented to the court over which Judge Wm. J. Bacon was presiding, S. S. Morgan district attorney. The indictments charged Asa Fuller, Hill Davis, Wm. Dutcher, Ernest Vance and Chas. Vance with assaulting and killing a saloon keeper or a hotel landlord by the name of Campbell, at or near Frankfort Hill. The prisoners all plead guilty of manslaughter in the 2nd degree, and were sentenced to Auburn prison at hard labor for seven years each. Fuller, Davis and Dutcher were from Utica, the two Vances being residents of Frankfort.

The Lyman Poisoning Case, 1869

On Wednesday, December 8th, 1869, Mrs. Nancy
Lyman was brought up for trial before Judge H. A.
Foster, Chas. G. Burrows district attorney, who on the
trial was assisted by Judge Hardin. Mrs. Lyman was
indicted for poisoning her husband, Ephraim Gardner, at
Denison's Corners, a pretty little hamlet some distance
south of the village of Mohawk. While the belief was
general that the woman was guilty of the crime as
charged, the district attorney failed to find proof, and the
jury in consequence were obliged to give in a verdict of
acquittal. The prisoner was defended by the Hon. Sam'l
Earl and the Hon. Robert Earl. The post mortem
examination of the body revealed the presence of white
arsenic in sufficient quantity to produce death. How or
when the poison was administered remained a veiled
secret until after the trial. It was then claimed by some
that the deadly powder was given in a pie. The woman is
still living.

The Murder of William Eacker
by John A. Walrath, 1870

On the 30th day of November, 1870, the grand jury
presented to the court of Oyer and Terminer a true bill of
indictment for manslaughter, against John A. Walrath,
for the killing of one William Eacker.

The murder took place in the town of Manheim, on
the 25th day of November. According to the indictment
Eacker came to his death by being severely beaten and
kicked.

The case was sent to the Sessions for trial, and finally
came up before Judge Amos H. Prescott, on February
20th, 1872. The district attorney, A. M. Mills, was
assisted on the trial by A. B. Steele. H. Clay Hall
appeared as counsel for the defense, assisted by the able
criminal lawyer, S. S. Morgan.

The affray in which Eacker met his death, occurred at
Ingham's Mills. The deceased, after the fight, made his
way along a dark passage, and was discovered dead on
the large flag stone just before the door. Near the body
was found a small stone, which the district attorney
claimed that Walrath had used in committing the deed. It
was suggested by others that H. Clay Hall placed it there
in order to form a theory for the defense, but no attention
was paid to the remark.

In order to prove that a skull could be easily fractured
on the side above the ear, the district attorney presented
in open court, the skull of a young woman, and
introduced it as evidence. H. Clay Hall on the
succeeding day presented the skull of a man of the same
age as Eacker, and proved to the satisfaction of the jury,
that it was impossible to fracture a skull of that age, with
the same ease as that of the young woman which the
district attorney had introduced. In spite of the efforts of
his counsel, the prisoner was found guilty, and sentenced
to State prison for two years.

Following his description of this case, Tippetts included a piece of what he called a "unique specimen of ghastly literature" written by one of the jurymen. That work, entitled "Dialogue of the Skulls" may be found as an appendix to the present volume.

- editor

The Murder of Alvah A. Avery
by Theodore Thompson, 1870

A desperate affray took place on October 1st, 1870, in the town of Salisbury, between Alvah Avery and Theodore Thompson. Avery and Thompson met at a hotel owned by H. J. Palmer, and from words finally proceeded to blows. During the melee Thompson succeeded in opening a large dirk knife and with it stabbed Avery in the upper part of the thigh. He was observed by persons present to rise suddenly from the floor, close the knife and make for the door. Before they hardly realized what had happened he made his escape across the bridge into Fulton county. It is reported by those cognizant of the affair that he visited his home and hurriedly said good-bye to his wife and family, saying that he was bound for Canada. He was not arrested, and consequently the case does not appear on the records.

Coroner Charles H. Batchelder, of Herkimer, was summoned to the scene of the crime, and impanneled a jury who, after hearing the testimony, rendered a verdict of murder against Thompson.

John T. Johnson and
Thomas McCallaghan , 1871

On March 30th, 1871, John T. Johnson and Thomas McCallaghan were brought into court under an indictment charging them jointly with murder. They pleaded not guilty and were remanded to jail to await trial. On March 31st, Johnson was brought before Judge Doolittle, Albert M. Mills, district attorney, and was allowed to enter a plea of guilty of manslaughter in the fourth degree. The plea was accepted by the Court, and he received a sentence of two years in the Onondaga Penitentiary. On April 6th, Callaghan pled guilty of murder in the second degree, and was sentenced to Auburn for seven years. The prisoners were charged with beating and kicking an unknown man to death on the 22d day of March, 1871.

John Foster and Edward Fleming, 1871

On Wednesday, July 5th, 1871, John Foster and
Edward Fleming, of Little Falls, were tried for the
murder of Anson Casler. The victim was beaten and
kicked to death. The case was called before Judge
Doolittle; Albert M. Mills, district attorney. After a
courts' session of a week's duration, Foster
was found not guilty, and Fleming discharged without a
trial.

The main point of evidence presented by the
prosecution was the statement of a convict from Auburn,
who, at the time of Foster's confinement in the Herkimer
jail, occupied the same cell as the prisoner. This witness
stated that Foster had admitted the killing to him. The
Court allowed the evidence, but the jury did not believe
the statement, and accordingly acquitted the prisoner.

Murder and Suicide of Husband, 1871
The Killing of Mrs. Pangburn by Her Husband

During the month of August, 1871, another horrible murder and suicide startled the quiet denizens of the Mohawk Valley, and, as usual, proved the chief topic of conversation for a longer period than the proverbial nine days. The murder referred to happened on or about the 15th day of August, and before daylight in the morning, of East Frankfort.

The neighbors living near were aroused from their quiet matutinal slumbers by a series of frenzied shrieks issuing from the house of Dyer Pangburn. On entering a terrible sight met their eyes. Mrs. Pangburn was found in the kitchen with her head crushed and lying in a crimson pool of her own life blood. Near by was discovered a potato-masher, covered with blood, which had evidently been used to commit the deed.

The children, when questioned, stated "that their father was the murderer." A search of the premises was immediately instituted. On entering the barn the body of the husband--murderer and suicide--was found suspended from a beam. He was at once cut down, but life was extinct. Coroner Sheldon, of Frankfort, was summoned and held an inquest, the verdict of the jury being in accordance with the above facts.

The Dykeman Murder, 1874

Alfred Travers Dykeman was indicted for murder on the 28th day of April, 1874. The case came up for trial, May 8th, before Judge George A. Hardin. Albert M. Mills, district attorney, assisted by Judge George W. Smith, appeared for the people. After a court session of nearly a week the jury returned a verdict of guilty in the first degree, and the prisoner was sentenced to be hung on the 25th day of June. The criminal was ably defended by J. A. & A. B. Steele, who, on the 22d day of May, agreed with the district attorney upon a bill of exceptions, and carried the case to the General Term for argument. On the 23d of June, J. A. Steele argued for a new trial before the General Term at Buffalo, and secured a reversal of the conviction. The second trial of Dykeman began on November 17th, and was of about the same duration. The jury found the prisoner guilty of murder in the second degree, and Dykeman was sentenced to State prison for life.

The murder for which Dykeman was sentenced was the killing of Benj. Dykeman, in the town of Warren, near what is known as the Cruger Mansion. It is supposed that Alfred Dykeman, the prisoner, was guilty of criminal intimacy with his victim's wife; that Benjamin Dykeman, the murdered man, came up from Mohawk and found Alfred with her, and that a desperate quarrel thereupon ensued. The killing was universally admitted, but it was claimed that the prisoner stabbed him in self-defense.

Lorenzo Hays, 1874

Lorenzo Hays was indicted for the murder of Norman R. P. Bellinger, September, 1874. The case came up for trial at the Court of Sessions, before Judge Amos H. Prescott, but as a prisoner under indictment for murder cannot be tried in this court, Judge Prescott referred the case to the next Oyer and Terminer.

At the term of Oyer and Terminer which convened on November 20th, Hays was brought before Judge George A. Hardin, and withdrew his plea of not guilty, and plead guilty of manslaughter in the 4th degree. The court accepted the plea, and Hays was sentenced to the county jail for one year, and to pay a fine of $250. At the end of his term of imprisonment, Hays was brought from jail on a writ of habeas corpus, and an error being found in the wording of the fine, discharged from custody.

The crime for which the prisoner was tried, was the killing of Bellinger on August 4th, 1874, at Little Falls. The deceased was found dead, with a terrible wound in the head, back of the right ear. Albert M. Mills, as district attorney, conducted the case for the people, H. Clay Hall appearing for the defense.

The Murder of Orlo Davis, 1875
By the Fredenburgs, in the Town of Ohio

The murder of Orlo Davis, in the town of Ohio, on the 23rd day of June, 1875, is well remembered by the people of Herkimer county. The case created considerable excitement at the time, and the trial, in the following November, was largely attended.

On November 8th of the same year, before Judge Milton H. Merwin, appeared Lodicia Fredenburg, Albert Fredenburg, Mary Davis and Franklin Davis, to answer the charge of murder. As the Fredenburgs had no counsel, S. S. Morgan was assigned by the court, Judge George W. Smith acting
as counsel for the Davis. On November 20th, district attorney Albert M. Mills brought up the case, and after a long session, the Fredenburgs were found guilty of murder in the first degree. The court sentenced them to be hung December 31st, between the hours of ten and four.

The testimony produced at the trial proved that the Fredenburgs killed Davis by striking him on the neck with an ax. On April 26th, Albert Fredenburg was respited by the Governor, until a motion could be made for a new trial. After hearing the argument the court took the papers and
reserved decision. On April 29th, Judge Hardin decided against a new trial, and stated that the sentence of the court must be carried out. The two Davis's were allowed to give state's evidence, and were finally discharged from custody on motion of their counsel, the Hon. George W. Smith.

Immediately after the sentence a strong effort was made in behalf of the prisoners. An affidavit was secured from Mary Davis, to the effect that the testimony given by her on the trial was false. When the papers were presented to Governor Tilden, and he had looked them over, he stated "That he would not hang a dog on such testimony," and commuted the sentence of death to imprisonment for life. It is reported that Mrs. Fredenburg died on Blackwell's Island abort one year ago, and that Albert, after remaining some time as an inmate of Auburn prison was transferred to Clinton.

The Murder of Mulverhill at Newport, 1876

The murder of Mulverhill by Pat Crowley, in 1876,
created as much excitement in the county as any
previous case. The evidence produced at the
trial by the prosecution proved in every way that the
homicide was a premeditated and cold-blooded murder.
Mulverhill was a brother-in-law of the murderer, having
married his sister. The marriage for some reason or other
proved distasteful to Crowley, and he upon several
occasions had evinced a desire to quarrel with his
brother-in-law.

On the day of the murder Crowley was at home,
engaged in the laudable occupation of sampling the
contents of a keg of hard cider. As the sampling process
proceeded, Crowley gradually became elevated, and was
soon in a condition to engage in anything from a free
fight to a murder. While in this delicious frame of mind
he looked out of the window and perceived his brother-
in-law driving by in a sleigh. The sight enraged Crowley
to such an extent that he sprang through the doorway,
seized a stick of wood and ran up the road after the
cutter. Mulverhill stopped the sleigh and waited
for his brother-in-law to approach. Crowley came up,
and without haying a word struck Mulverhill a terrible
blow on the head, killing him almost instantly.

The murderer was arrested and indicted for the crime,
April 18th, 1876. The case came up for trial before
Judge George A. Hardin, April 26th, but was postponed
until next Court, May 7th, 1877. As the peculiarities of
law are past the ken of mortal man., the case did not
come up until December 11th, 1877, when it was tried
before Judge Milton H. Merwin. The prisoner was found
guilty of murder in the second degree, and sentenced to
State prison for life.

The case for the people was conducted by J. J.
Dudleston, Jr., assisted by the previous district attorney,
A. M. Mills. The prisoner was defended by the late S. S.

Morgan, one of the best criminal lawyers ever known in this County.

Mulverhill's skull, which was introduced in Court, is now in an upper chamber--over the judges' room--in the Court House, at Herkimer.

The Shooting of Moses Holden
by Alphonzo Klock, 1880

Alphonzo Klock, of Little Falls, was indicted for shooting Moses Holden, on November 11th, 1880. The case was tried before Judge Milton H. Mervin,--A. B. Steele, district attorney,--on February 14th, 1881. The jury retired, and brought in a verdict of manslaughter in the third degree, but
strongly recommending the prisoner to the mercy of the Court. He was sentenced to two years in State prison, and served his term.

The facts of the murder are as follows: Moses C. Holden, a married man and resident of Herkimer, became acquainted with Klock's sister, and finally succeeded in seducing her. They afterwards lived together, both in Herkimer and Syracuse. The woman, after giving birth to a child, of which Holden was the undoubted father, was finally persuaded to leave him, and again returned home. Holden was seen in the neighborhood on several different occasions, and was as often warned to keep away. He paid no attention to the warning, and one night was discovered by the brother in the barn attached to the premises. The barn being dark in the interior Klock was unable to distinguish features, but as he stepped towards the dark corner in which he had observed the moving figure, Holden walked towards him, at the same time ordering him to leave the place, or he would compel him. Klock claims that Holden raised his arm as though about to strike, and that he thereupon drew his revolver and fired one shot. Holden uttered a cry, sprang through the open door of the barn and dropped dead a few paces away.

The shooting took place Sunday night and the body was allowed to remain exposed to the rays of a hot summer sun until late Monday afternoon. Klock went to Little Falls the next morning and gave himself up.

As the recommendation of the jury bears witness, the sympathy of the public was largely in favor of the prisoner. He was defended by the able criminal lawyer, S. S. Morgan, and to his eloquent argument can in a measure owe his short sentence.

John Welch Kills His Wife
at Little Falls, 1882

John Welch, a stonemason by trade and the proprietor of a saloon at Little Falls known as Washington Hall, was indicted on February 13d, 1882, for the murder of his wife:

The particulars of the murder are as follows: Welch was intoxicated at the time and asked his wife for a bottle of whiskey which she had procured for him a short time before. She replied "that she knew nothing about it." Welch told her that she lied, and aimed a blow at her head. The woman escaped the blow and ran through two or three rooms, the prisoner following in pursuit. A little son of the pair told his father that his mother had hidden the bottle under a pillow in the bedroom. Welch, after a search secured the whiskey, and then proceeded to beat and illtreat his wife in so brutal a manner that she bled to death.

The case was brought before the next term of Court for trial. The Court convened May 31st, 1882, with Judge Irvine G. Vann on the bench, and A. B Steele, district attorney. After a long session the jury brought in a verdict of murder in the second degree, and the prisoner was accordingly sentenced to State prison for life. S. S. Morgan, the counsel for the defendant, moved for a new trial, but the Court denied the motion.

The case was afterwards appealed to the General Term, but after a hearing the conviction was sustained. During the trial the prosecution offered to prove that Welch and his wife had some seven or eight years previous, murdered her first husband John Horan by name. The woman was reported as confessing the crime to a neighbor, and at the same time expressing an apprehension that Welch would kill her in the near future. The aim of the district attorney was to secure a conviction of murder in the first degree.

Drs. Draper and Suiter performed a special post mortem examination, which evinced the fact that two or three ribs were broken, and that there was a strong probability that the woman came to her death from concussion of the heart or brain. It was finally decided not to press the matter, as the Court declined to receive the evidence, assigning as a reason subsequently, that by so doing the jury would have convicted the prisoner of murder in the first degree, while the testimony presented in regard to the present murder, did not warrant a conviction only in the second.

Mrs. Parkes, of Herkimer, Kills Her Two Children and Then Commits Suicide, 1883

The particulars of this terrible tragedy are gathered from the account published at the time, in the Utica Daily Observer. The article was written by our popular young townsman, Judge T. C. Murray, to whom the writer is indebted for favors which he taken this occasion to acknowledge. The triple murder occurred on the evening of Sunday, March 25th, 1883, at the residence of the unfortunate woman, on Prospect street, Herkimer. The following is Mr. Murray's account of the affair:

HERKIMER, March 26.

The most horrible tragedy ever enacted in this vicinity occurred here about 8:40 P. M. Sunday. The facts as nearly as could be ascertained by your correspondent are substantially as follows

Thomas Parkes is a member of the firm of Parkes, Barry & Co., grocers and druggists of this place. His family consisted of a wife and two children, the oldest child about five years of age, and the youngest an infant of about two months. Mrs. Parkes was an estimable lady, about 25 years old, and is a sister of the wife of Jerome L. Farrington, who lives near the Ilion depot. Mr. Parkes was, until his removal here, about a year ago, an employee of the Remingtons, holding a responsible position as book-keeper. Last evening the whole community was horrified by the news which spread like wild fire, that Mrs. Parkes had shot herself and two children. The news proved, on investigation, only too true. The facts as learned from the lips of those who know most of the terrible tragedy, are as follows

Between 8 and 9 o'clock Mrs. Parkes, who was in bed or about to prepare for bed, called the servant girl and told her to summon Mrs. Bull, who lives in the next house, as she wanted to see her. The girl immediately left the house, and after delivering leer message, came directly back, and found
Mrs. Parkes lying on the bed, a child on either side. Mrs. Parkes grasped a pistol in her right hand, a wound from which appeared on her right temple, and both children were gasping in death, from a wound in the head from the pistol in the hands of the mother.

The girl had not been from the house ten minutes, and the result which appeared had been accomplished apparently with the greatest deliberation. The mother had lain down on the bed between the two children, and shot them first, as they lay, the ball in each case entering the side of the head next to her. She then placed the still smoking weapon to her own head, and discharged the contents of another barrel into her brain. The mother died almost immediately after receiving her wound. The youngest child lived about three hours, and the oldest one died about four o'clock this morning.

Of course, as is always the case upon the enactment of such a horrible tragedy, which no one could foresee, and which there was apparently no possible reason for, the air is full of rumors as to the circumstances that drove this unfortunate woman to such a desperate deed. Her sanity has never been questioned, and to all appearances her domestic relations were the pleasantest. But many are now ready with, " I told you so," and, " Just as I expected," &c. Stories of neglect, and ill treatment by the husband are rife. Mr. Parkes was not at home when the shooting occurred, and could not be found for a couple of hours, a circumstance which gives rise to ugly rumors.

Coroner Suiter impanneled the following jury on Monday, March 26th, and held an inquest, at the Court House: E. B. Mitchell, foreman; Isaac F. Small, George-H. Gray, S. W. Stimson, Smith C. Harter, Win. H. Prowse, A. C: Devendorf, Wm. H. Fiske, Sheriff Brown. The coroner examined a number of witnesses, among the number Mr. Thomas Parkes, the husband. Mr. Parkes at the inquest evinced great grief over the affair, and proved to the complete satisfaction of the large audience present that his love for the deceased was great, and his grief profound. He proved also that he was in no wise to blame, and received the sympathy of all that heard his. testimony.

The following is the verdict of the coroner's jury: "The jury find that Mrs. Eugenia Parkes came to her death from the effects of a pistol shot wound inflicted by her own hand, on the 25th day of March, 1883, between the hours of 8 and 9 p.m., at her residence in the village of Herkimer, N. Y. We further find and certify that at the time she inflicted said wounds, she was laboring under temporary mental abberation. The jury also find that Lulu Parkes and Infant Parkes came to their death from the effect of a pistol shot wound inflicted upon each of them, on the 25th day of March, 1883, by their mother, Mrs. Eugenia Parkes, at her residence in the village of Herkimer, N. Y., and that the said Lulu Parkes died on the morning of the 26th of March, at one o'clock; and we further find and certify that at the time of the infliction of said wounds, said Mrs. Eugenia Parkes was laboring under temporary mental abberation."

Sarah Culver Indicted
for Killing Her Infant Child, 1884

On April 24th, 1884, Miss Sarah Culver was indicted for the murder of her illegitimate infant child. The case came up for trial before Judge Geo. N. Kennedy, September 8th, 1884. District attorney A. B. Steele conducted the case for the prosecution, Judge George W. Smith appearing for the defendant. Judge Smith labored hard to secure an acquittal, summed up in a masterly manner, and delivered a plea that evidently captured the jury, as that body rendered a verdict completely exonerating his client.

The testimony in this case was of the most conflicting nature, and it is hard to say whether or not a crime was committed. To the best of my belief, from hearing reports of the testimony, the accused was innocent of the crime, the charge probably arising from slanders circulated by a miserable set of meddlesome busy-bodies. The child very likely died naturally immediately after birth, and as the little one was ushered into the world with the brand of illegitimacy stamped upon its forehead, it was after all, perhaps, the best thing that could have happened under the circumstances. The only fault I am able to discover was the concealment of the infant's birth and death. In order that the child's advent into life might not become bruited abroad, the body was buried in the cellar, where the bones were afterwards found.

Sufficient testimony was not found to insure a conviction, and in the opinion of many now resident of Herkimer, the woman was justly acquitted:

The Murder of John Wishart,
Near Frankfort 1884
The Italian, Frank Mondon, and
the Two Wisharts Held for the Crime

The body of John Wishart was found, May 8th, 1884, on that portion of the Mohawk flats east of Frankfort, owned by Sanford Getman. The corpse was discovered in a ditch by the murdered man's son, Adam Wishart, who for some time had been engaged in searching for the remains. On the right side of the head was a long, deep cut, resembling a wound inflicted by some sharp instrument. Nearby was found a broken club, bearing stains of blood, with shreds of skin and a few hairs attached.

John Wishart was a German, over 70 years of age, and lived about a quarter of a mile west of the N. Y. Central depot at Frankfort, and in the town of Schuyler. He was last seen alive in the village of East Schuyler, about three weeks before the finding of the remains. He had not lived happily with his family, consisting of his wife, two sons, two daughters, and their husbands. As he had a daughter in Utica and a son in Syracuse, it was supposed by some that he had gone to one of those cities, and nothing strange was thought of his absence. About a week before the finding of the corpse inquiries were made in Utica and Syracuse, when it was learned that he had not been seen in either place. The people of the town began to surmise that Wishart had been foully dealt with, and a search being instituted, the body was found, as already stated.

Three of Wishart's daughters were married to Italians. The youngest, Louise, had recently married against her father's wishes and, as her husband, Frank Mondon, had been heard to utter threats against the old man's life, suspicion very naturally pointed towards him as the criminal. It is reported that the mother favored the marriage, while the father did all in his power to prevent it. John Wishart was looked upon by every one as a temperate, industrious, and kindly disposed man. He worked as a farm laborer whenever he could get work, and as soon as the job was finished and he had received his pay he would return home, and be kindly treated as long as the money lasted. Home, from being the dearest place on earth, became to him a perfect hell. At least such is the report. His son, Adam, who found the remains, is reported to have taken his father's part, and treated. him kindly.

Immediately after the discovery of the body, district attorney A. B. Steels, and Coroner Robert Warner, of Ilion, were notified, and went to Frankfort that same evening. Soon after, Deputy Sheriff Delos V. Finster and Police Constable A. Frank Clark, of Frankfort, began a search for Mondon. The supposed murderer was found at the Wishart house, in bed, and owing to the peculiar reputation of other members of the family, it was deemed advisable to arrest Mondon's wife, Louise, Mrs. Nancy Wishart, the widow, some 60 years of age, and a son, Frederick, and his wife. Officer Sylvester Wilson made the arrests, and on informing Mrs. Wishart that the Italian was wanted, she asked: "What for?" Officer Clark told her that her husband's dead body had been found, and she thereupon burst into tears. Her daughter, Mondon's wife, proceeded to comfort her by exclaiming: "What the h-1 are you crying about? You must be sick to cry over that old fool."

The officers took their prisoners to Frankfort, where they were arraigned before Justice Ingham and committed. Mondon was placed in the lockup and the others held in custody at the Central Hotel.

Coroner Warner impanneled the following jury, and proceeded to hold an inquest: Sanford Getman, foreman, J. L. Osgood, W: Durst, W: Campbell, Edward Haner; Eugene Klock, John Krick, and Jesse Kingsbury.

Drs. G. N. Lehr and W. H. H. Parkhurst, both of Frankfort, made a post mortem examination. The inquest commenced at six o'clock, Thursday, and continued until Saturday afternoon, when it was adjourned untilMonday. The prisoners remained in jail in Herkimer, under the care of Sheriff Brown, over Sunday.

The following is a brief synopsis of the testimony elicited by the coroner

Sanford Getman

"It was about three weeks ago that I last saw the deceased alive; on Thursday last I saw Adam Wishart running down the flats; I asked him what the matter was? He replied: "My father is down there in the ditch, dead"; I went there and found the body; Adam told me that the Italian, Mondon, had threatened to kill his father three or four times; I had let them have some land to work there; John Wishart at present had no home, as I understood that the family had turned him out of the house; Wishart told me so himself; I do not know where he stayed after he was turned out; the place where the body lay was not frequented by people; noticed a cut on the head; a man standing in the ditch could not be seen from any of the houses near, because of bushes growing on the side; Wishart at one time told me that his wife had threatened to kill him; she kicked him out doors; that he slept on the floor and they did not give him any covering; never saw him drink or heard of his drinking."

Adam Wishart

"Am a son of the deceased, and last saw him alive about three weeks ago, on the creek bridge, in the afternoon; don't remember what he said; he had lived very unhappily at home; Mondon and my sister had been

56

married about four months; father told me that the Italian had threatened his life; that Mondon said that he would catch him on the bridge some dark night and throw him into the river; I have been searching for him since Monday; I had my suspicions that he had been killed; I started for the village to procure hooks to drag the river; my sister, Julia Coach, told me to go along by Getman's and look there; I went and found the body; I did not say anything to the Italian about it, as I was afraid he would run away before the officers could arrest him; I have had trouble with my mother; I told her, if they would put that Italian out, that father would provide for the family; she ordered me to mind my own business; I saw part of an envelope near the body, picked it up and gave it to my wife; don't know whether father had any money with him."

At the request of the district attorney, witness asked his wife for the envelope, but she replied that she had burned it.

" I recognized the body by the pants and boots, before I saw the face; had no reason to believe that the body was there; did not hear my brothers and sisters, living at home, make any inquiry .about father's absence."

Mrs. Nancy Hagen

Said that "she last saw deceased coming down the railroad track from his house; two men were with him, dressed in grayish clothes; don't know them; don't know the Italian who married Louise; the men stepped over Getman's fence and went down the river; one had a hack cap; did not notice the other one; about the same height; Adam Wishart was not one of them; did not see them come lack; did not see an axe or anything with them; don't know the day of the week; know it was not Sunday."

Frank Mondon

"The Italian accused of the murder, testified as follows:
Have been an this country two years; lived at Frankfort
ten or eleven months; worked on West Shore tracks;
lived with Mr. Wishart two or three months; married his
daughter, Louise; John Wishart was at home last time
four or five weeks ago; one of the brothers said John had
gone to Syracuse; saw him go to Michael Coach's; he did
not come back; John had no trouble with me; Will and
John had a fight one night when Louise and I were in
bed; Will wanted to fight with me; I did not go down the
river with John; don't know where John went.

A club formed from the dried limb of a tree and broken
in two pieces, was shown witness. Being asked if he
killed John with that? he replied

"Me stay nota in this place if me fixes John with that; me
no, go backs to Wishat's."

Michael Coach

An Italian son-in-law of Wishart's, testified: Been in this
country nine and one-half years; work on railroad; saw
Wishart last alive, three weeks ago on bridge near the
house; he stayed with me when he could not get in his
own house; he said that his life had been threatened by
Frank; about four months ago Frank said he would give
old John a good licking; Wishart never liked Frank; I did
not try to find body, as I have been out of town looking
for work; have not been in Wishart's house for three or
four months; heard Mrs. Wishart say about four months
ago that she did not want him around; have heard Louise
tell him to get out of the house; haven't spoken to Louise
since she was married.

Joe Frank

Another Italian son-in-law was called as interpreter, and
Frank again put on the stand: I saw John last three weeks
ago, in front of house, on railroad bridge; a German was
with him; have seen the German since in Frankfort;
don't know his name; he wore a black cap and had a
black moustache; never saw these clubs before; never
did Wishart any harm; don't know anything about who
killed him; never threatened to lick the old man; never
told Coach.I would.

Alonzo Wishart

A son of deceased: Lives at Coach's; saw father last
three weeks ago; was at home one night during past two
weeks; asked where father was; didn't ask mother; didn't
ask Louise; have not much to say to her; heard about the
finding of father's body on Thursday afternoon; did not
tell them at the house; I didn't help put my father in the
ditch; heard my sister say the body must be there; it was
talked over a couple of days; didn't know why Michael
did not go down with Adam; guess he was afraid.

District attorney--Afraid that he would find the body?

Witness, nodding his head and laughing--I guess so;
never heard father say he didn't want Louise to marry
Frank; Louise said she wanted him and she got him;
don't know how old I am; only went to school four
weeks; don't know whether father and the boys ever had
trouble.

Mrs. Hattie Wishart

Wife of Adam: Last saw deceased three weeks ago; he
brought flour to our house, and I baked bread for him

next day; he talked of going to Syracuse; was at father's house but once since Louise was married; heard Frank say once, "G-d d-n him, we'll fix him in one lick;" Mike and John were present at the time; the only time I ever heard him threaten father; don't understand much that he says; Adam said Thursday morning, he didn't see where father could be, and I suggested that he look for him, where he had been working.

The inquest then adjourned until Monday. On Monday it was resumed, and then adjourned until Friday. The knife of Wishart was found on the Italian; it was also proved that he and Wishart quarreled on the day he was missed, and that the Italian followed him down the railroad track.

Augustus Clifford

Testified that: He lives about 20 rods from the Wishart house; saw deceased last about 4 or 5 weeks ago; while passing the house on the 17th of April, in the afternoon, heard the voice of a woman crying; it was the most agonizing cry I ever heard; I heard a voice crying, "Oh they have killed "; don't know whose voice it was; saw Alonzo Faulkner and his sister pass the house; asked - them what the matter was; he replied, "Oh, they are having one of their spells at the Wishart house; when I looked back Mrs. Wishart was standing in the doorway; still heard the same voice crying; don't think it was Louise; it was a woman's voice; I had not seen John Wishart that day or since.

Mrs. Nancy Wishart

The widow, testified substantially as follows: "Last saw my husband about four weeks ago; do not remember of standing in the doorway on Thursday morning; was not at home at that time; Frank Mondon was crying in the barn several days before; he and his wife, Louise, had, some words and he struck her with a stick; Mondon was jealous, and twitted her about an Italian she met last fall; he told her she could have the Italian if she wanted to; she replied that she didn't have to; she then called him a - - - - ; he would not take that, and struck her across the back, twice, with a switch; I heard Mr. Clifford say that he heard crying; I did not hear it when at the house; Mondon often had crying spells in the barn, in fact he rarely did anything else but cry; Louise and Frank occasionally had Words about men and women; the first time he struck her was before the old man went away; they often twitted one another, and afterwards she would go to the bedroom and he would follow her; they would remain half an hour, and after they came out she would be just as pleasant as ever; Frank would cry because of his jealousy, I did not see Mr. Clifford pass the house; I saw Mr. Faulkner and his sister pass the house; John stayed in the house that night; I saw the old man the next week after we gave the dance, on the Monday night following Easter Sunday; he was at the house in the morning; started west on Thursday; the old man asked me to bake bread; the last morning I saw him we had a few words, and he then left and went west; I went out and milked; when I came back Bessie was the only one there; when Louise got up she wanted to know what the old man wanted; I told her he wanted bread; Frank had not come from the bedroom at the time; John had said that 'the Italian had a wife in Italy, and that he would be made to suffer some time; at no time during the morning did Frank see John; I was the first one up that morning; I saw him have a pocket-book last winter; he lost his knife, but bought another; Louise was crying in the room when Faulkner and his sister passed by; do not remember to have heard her say: "Oh they have killed "; she often had crying spells when Frank went away, and once said that she would kill herself; when Faulkner went by she said, "Oh, dear," or something like that; I don't know whether Lon was; think John was home the night Faulkner went by; I will not swear that Frank went

away the day that John did; I remember that Frank went to look for work the week that John was found; John came to the house the night of the dance; I went in the room where the dancing was; I was dancing with the Italian; John said we ought to be ashamed; John took three chairs and a water pail and placed them near the door; he pounded around by the door, and took a window light out; Fred took hold of John by the collar, and put him out and locked the door after him; I told him to; no one touched John except Fred; Frank knew of the disturbance, but was not near John; Frank did not raise a club at him; Lon was full and foolish, and wanted to get at him, but was held back by the Italians; when Fred went at the old man the music stopped, but the row did not break up the dance; Lon had often threatened the old man, but I never saw him strike him; never heard Frank threaten to strike him; have known Louise to misuse and throw stones at her father; all the children have had words with their father; at the house one day, when Frank went after water, Louise followed him and John followed her; John struck at Frank with a club, but Louise caught the force of the blow; Frank wanted to get at the old man then, but Louise held him;
no one held the old man; Frank said to Louise: "Let me go"; Louise said: "Don't you fix any fight for the old man," and Frank said that he wouldn't."

The club found near the murdered man's body was exhibited, but Mrs. Wishart denied that it was the one about to be used at the time.

"There was no fuss between me and my husband after he found me in the cellar with men; he twitted me about it, and I told him it was none of his business; John slept up stairs; I have not slept with him since New Year's."

District attorney Steele: " Mrs. Wishart, will you swear that your husband was not killed in the house?"

"Yes, sir; I am as innocent of this crime as a child two years old; I did not say that the "dirty old toad had gone off with his clothes on;" did not hear Louise say that she wished the old cuss was dead; at the time of my arrest, I did not slap Frank on the shoulder and say, "They have found old John;" Louise did not say, "Mother, don't cry about the old fool;" I did not know what I was arrested for."

This concluded her testimony. Several times during the examination she appeared worried and perspired so exceedingly, that she was kept busy wiping the perspiration from her face. The woman is very cunning, and undoubtedly knows more about the killing of her husband than she is willing to admit.

On Saturday evening the jury handed in the following verdict

"On the 17th day of April, 1884, at the town of Schuyler, in said county of Herkimer, one Frank Mondon did strike the said John Wishart with a club or other heavy instrument, which he then and there held in his hand, feloniously and with malice aforethought, and with intent to kill the said John Wishart, and that the said Frank Mondon, at the time and place aforesaid, wilfully, feloniously, and of malice aforethought, the said John Wiahart did kill and murder; and the jurors aforesaid, upon their oaths, do further say that Nancy Wishart and Louise Mondon abetted, aided and counseled the said Frank Mondon in the commission of the said offense, and in the killing and murdering of the said John Wishart, at the time and in the manner above set forth."

Among other witnesses were Alonzo Wishart, Mike Coach, Harris Lewis, Alonzo M. Lintz, Fred Wishart,

Louise Mondon, Sheriff Brown, E. H. Minott, Alonzo
Faulkner, Horace Ingham, James H. J. Watkins.

The result of the post mortem and the finding of the
clubs make the case beyond a doubt, one of murder. The
head bore marks of a severe blow from behind, causing a
fracture of the skull on the left side. On the club picked
up near by, were found a few hairs, corresponding in
color to that of the deceased. On one of the pieces is a
sort of knot or place where a branch had been out off,
which exactly fitted an indentation in the back of the
head.

The Wishart family, who were examined as
witnesses, can neither read or write, and some of them
did not understand the nature of an oath. The Italian
speaks but very little English, and it was hard for the
coroner to understand his testimony.

After the conclusion of the inquest the prisoners were
taken to Herkimer jail, where they now remain in charge
of Sheriff Brown.

At a session of the grand jury, in the following
November, that body found a true bill of murder in the
first degree against the Italian, and indicted Nancy
Wishart as accessory. The case went over the term, and
will some up for trial this present term of court.

As Mondon had no counsel the court assigned ex-
District Attorney J. J. Dudleston, Jr. Mr. Dudleston is a
good lawyer, and will do everything in his power to
assure a verdict of acquittal.

Mrs. Nancy Wishart retained the Hon. S. S. Morgan
as counsel, but as that celebrated criminal lawyer is
lately deceased, she has now assured the services of
Dexter E. Pomeroy, of Utica. Mr. Pomeroy is a well
known lawyer, and is possessed of a clear head, good
legal knowledge and excellent judgment. District
attorney Steele will conduct the case for the people, and
as all are equally confident of success, the trial is sure to
prove an interesting one. No indictment was found

against Louis, the Italian's wife, but she is still retained, as a witness, at the county jail.

1884 Was it Murder?

The Mysterious Disappearance of Chas. R. Derby, from the Village of Ilion.
Chas. R. Derby, a well known collector and accountant, disappeared from the village of Ilion during the month of November, 1884.

Derby was an inoffensive man, his only fault being a too great fondness for spirituous liquors. His chief occupation was acting as collector for different merchants of the town, and also posting their books, as often as the necessities of the ease seemed to demand. Derby was often known to have in his possession large sums of money, but as his honesty was unquestionable, his continued absence at length aroused the suspicion of his friends. Various conjectures, of one kind and another, were made in regard to his whereabouts. It was reported that he had been seen at different points in the west, but an inquiry being made the reports were found to be without a basis of fact. It was said that his financial matters were perfectly straight, and those delightful mortals who prefer a choice bit of gossip to anything else in the world, were therefore forced to change their theory of his absence.

All doubts were rudely dispelled on Tuesday forenoon, December the 2d. When the water of the Erie Canal was drawn off for the winter, all that was mortal of poor Charlie Derby was found in its muddy bed. There is no doubt but that his body went into the canal at the lock west of Ilion, and that during its stay of two weeks in the water, it passed along to the place where it was found. As the canal had been thoroughly dragged it was strange that the remains were not found before.

The battered appearance of the corpse led to the arrest of one or more parties known to have been with Darby on the evening of his disappearance, but no one was retained or lodged in jail. The body on being found was taken to the rooms of Undertaker Chattaway and the following jury at once impanneled by Coroner Warner: S. T. Russell, foreman, W. J. Lewis, Fred Coleman, Joseph Summers, Wm. Onyans, J. B. Wilde, Alexander Jess, Joseph Taylor, J. K. P. Harris. Drs. Rasbach and Draper held an autopsy at the request of the coroner. The lungs were found full of air, showing that the victim had not met his death by drowning; this, with the fact that his money and watch and chain were missing, led to the arrests before mentioned.

The inquest commenced on Wednesday morning, at Justice Lester's office, and was adjourned until Friday. The evidence all proved that Darby had been last seen on or about November 18th, but no light was thrown upon the supposed murder. The following is the testimony of Dr. Rasbach, corroborated by Dr. E. M. Draper, the two physicians who performed the post mortem:

"I knew Darby; made a post mortem, assisted by Dr. Draper; found extensive fracture of bones of skull, laceration of the menengese covering the brain, laceration of the brain substance, fracture of both upper and lower jaw bones, fracture of the right thigh, and compound fracture of the left tibia and fibula; found the lungs fully inflated with air; no water in the bronchial tubes or in the air cells; the amount of air in the lungs was sufficient to buoy him; think the majority of the cuts on his head were received after he was in the water; I don't think that if he was drowned the lungs would be inflated with air; I don't believe that he respired after he entered the water; I think he received injuries before he was submerged, probably of the skull; don't think he could have received the injuries he had on the head through his hat; I should expect to find the lungs of a drowned person partially filled with water, or, if not, in a condition of collapse; I think falling on stone could have produced the injuries on the head, had he fallen fifteen feet; I would not expect to find that kind of injury from a club; I believe he died from surgical shock, due to extreme violence; before sub-mersion; I should judge the body had been in the water two weeks; the heart was not taken out, but it seemed large.'"

The evidence presented on Friday proved that Darby had money on his person, and also a good watch andchain when last seen. None of these were found upon him; and as the battered appearance of the body indicated foul play, the jury, after a short session returned with the following verdict:

"That in the opinion of this jury, Chas. R. Darby came to his death at the hands of some person or persons unknown to this jury, and that the body was afterwards thrown into the Erie Canal, between the store of J. C. Brizolara at East Frankfort and hawk locks, on or after the evening of the 18th day of November 1884."

Chas. H. Williams, a colored man, was arrested for the crime, but easily proved his innocence, and was honorably discharged. This murder-if indeed it can be called a murder-bids fair to remain forever veiled in impenetrable obscurity. It is supposed by many that Darby received his death by falling from the tow-path into the canal, his head accidentally coming in contact with a rock, and was probably dead before he struck the water.

The Druse Butchery, 1884

**The Most Horrible Murder, on Record. William
Druse, of Warren, Killed, Butchered. and the
Body Burned in Stoves. The Wife Daughter,
Son and Nephew Arrested for the Crime.**

Herkimer county, during the past few years, has been
gradually coming into prominence as the scene of
horrible murders. The annals of criminal history contain
many terrible crimes, but it was thought that every
known method of committing a homicide had long since
been exhausted. It remained for the little to town of
Warren to produce another feature and she has
responded in a way that leaves nothing to be desired by
people of a morbid turn of mind or lovers of the horrible.

The details of the crime are almost too terrible for
contemplation, but that the ends of justice may be
attained, and a full knowledge of the facts placed before
the public, I deem it best to present a true and
unvarnished statement of the affair.

In an old dingy yellow farm house, about a quarter of
a mile from the main road, and near the village of Little
Lakes, on the 18th day of last December, was committed
one of the most horrible murders known to the annals of
crime. Wm. Druse, a farmer 60 years of age, was shot,
and his body hacked to pieces by an infuriated wife and
her children.

Wm. Druse disappeared from home on the 18th day
of December. The day following his house was locked
up, none of the family seen about, and forth from the
chimney poured a dense black smoke, filling the air
around the place with a very offensive odor. A number
of the neighbors noticed the smoke at the time, and as
days rolled by, and Druse's absence became manifest,
curious surmises were made in regard to his
whereabouts. Surmises became rumors, rumors finally
became facts, and at last it was openly asserted that
Druse had been murdered.

At this stage of the proceedings, district attorney A. B. Steele, of Herkimer, was sent for, and on his arrival made acquainted with such facts as the neighbors had gleaned. Mr. Steele immediately caused the arrest of Frank Gates, nephew of the deceased, and by dint of severe cross-questioning, succeeded in compelling the youth to confess his participation in the murder. The district attorney at once telephoned to Dr. L.O. Nellie, one of the three coroners of this county; that gentleman arriving on the scene early Friday morning, January the 16th. As the boy's confession implicated others, orders were given for the arrest of Roxy Druse, the wife, Mary Druse, a daughter, George Druse, a son, and on Saturday, Roxy Druse's brother-in-law, Chas. Gates.

The boy's confession is substantially as follows: he states, that Roxy after the old gentleman was through the morning chores, sent the two boys, Frank and George out of the room, and coming up behind Druse while he was seated at the breakfast table, fired one shot from a revolver into the back of his neck; two more shots were also fired by her, but their location at present is uncertain; she then called Frank in and placing the pistol at his head ordered him to complete the deed, threatening at the same time should he refuse, to kill him at once, he took the revolver and fired one shot into Druse's back. The supposition is, that Mary, the daughter, was at this time holding a rope that was fastened around her father's neck, and that she was the one that dragged him from the chair to the floor. After the last shot was fired Frank brought Mrs. Druse an ax, with which she struck her husband twice on the head, he exclaiming at the same time, "Oh, Roxy, don't! " The second blow probably killed him. as he never spoke again. The woman then severed the head from the body, and, as she said, threw it into the kitchen stove.

After the murder Frank brought from up stairs a large tick filled with straw, and assisted Mrs. Druse in placing the body of her dead husband upon it, and together they carried the corpse into the parlor. Frank and George were then sent down to the brush lot after a sharp ax. They returned with the article and gave it to the woman. The boys were kept busy bringing shingles with which hot fires were built in both the parlor and kitchen stoves. The murderess then took the sharp ax, a razor, a jack knife, a board and a chopping block. She carried these into the parlor, and there proceeded to dismember the body.

The arms were first cut off, and then the legs; she chopped the limbs into small pieces and .threw them into the parlor stove. The body was then placed on the block and hacked and cut until she was enabled to get all the pieces into the kitchen stove. Frank says the ashes and pieces of burned bone were carried by his aunt and himself the next day to Ball's swamp, distant about half a mile from the house.

The Druse family now under arrest, consist of Roxy Druse, about 45 years of age: The woman has black hair and eyes, pinched features, sallow complexion, and sharp hooked nose. She is about five feet four inches in height. Mary Druse, the daughter, is about 20 years old; George Druse, 10 years, and Frank Gates, a whole family in crime. They were first taken to the residence of Jeremiah Eckler, about one-quarter of a mile distant from the scene of the murder.

By the boy's confession Coroner Nellis was able to discover the nearly destroyed remains in Ball's swamp. He then impanneled the following coroner's jury: Chas. McRorie, foreman; Charles Pett, Chas. Bond, Geo. L. Rathburn, Alonzo Filkins, Rozelle Warren, James Hall, Frank Springer, and Chester Armstrong, all of the town of Warren. Coroner Nellis summoned Drs. A. D. Getman and W. P. Borland, of Richfield Springs, to examine the remains. These consisted. of the contents of a small box, a mass of dirt, wood ashes and small pieces of bone, all frozen together in a solid mass. There were about 18 to 20 small pieces of bone, from one inch to two inches long. The two patellae or knee caps, were found, as also the upper end of the left tibia or lower leg bone, showing two articular surfaces, thereby proving conclusively that the bones were human.

Mrs. Druse's brother-in-law, Chas. Gates, is claimed by some to be implicated, as she asserts that he assisted in the killing, firing several shots from his own revolver, and that the officers would find two kinds of bullets in the ashes, apparently forgetting she fact that lead would not long exist in a bullet form where there was a very hot fire. Drs. Getman and Borland were examined in regard to the ashes and bones being human. They testified that in their judgment the remains were those of a human body:

The coroner's inquest was until Saturday noon, the 17th, held in the Eckler cheese house. At that hour the coroner adjourned to the town hall at Little Lakes, in order to accommodate the large crowd that the proceedings had brought into town. District attorney A. B. Steels assisted the coroner in the examination of the witnesses. As the testimony is voluminous, and would take up more space than a work of this kind would warrant, I will condense the evidence into

A GENERAL STATEMENT.

Jeremiah Eckler.

Has lived in Warren 28 years; knew the deceased; knew that he was missing, and on December 18th saw black smoke pouring out of the chimney, and perceived a very bad odor. The forepart of January he asked Mrs. Druse where William was? She said; in New York; they quarreled frequently.

Charles Pett.

Live nears; knew that Druse was missing; saw dense black smoke on December 18th pouring out of chimney; went there first last Saturday; saw stoves; went there again asked where Druse, and told her of the reports that he had been murdered; she said they were false; saw new paper on walls; asked Gates boy where William was; he said, gone away; told Mrs. Druse a boy had found an ax; she said she supposed that the other tools were under the snow; on Thursday went to Herkimer and .brought the district attorney, A. B. Steele, to my house.

Wm. Eckler.

Son of Jeremiah Eckler: Remembers smoke; color dark, bad smell, like burned meat; have heard no threats made by Mrs. Druse against her husband.

Fred Vrooman.

Found an ax in mill pond, near the bridge, (ax shown); it is the same ax; it was wrapped in a copy of the N. Y. weekly Tribune; no name on paper; got it out next day.

Alonzo Filkins.

Knew Druse; went to house. Thursday afternoon, after a hay knife he borrowed; knocked at the door, but could not got in; newspapers up at windows; heard talking inside; could not see in; went last evening about 9 o'clock, and found burned remains in Ball's swamp; carried them to Chas. Pett's. The party who informed us went direct to place and pointed out the substance we brought away; it was lightly covered with snow.

Frank Gates worked at Druse's for his board. The district attorney then asked Frank Gates if he was willing to tell all that he knew in reference to the murder, without any promise on the part of the people. He answered, " Yes, sir," and was told to proceed, which he did as follows, substantially.

Frank Gates

Last summer Mrs. Druse and Mary wanted to hire me to
shoot Druse; they said they would give me a good many
dollars for doing it; I told them I would not; there was
nothing more said, but this winter Mrs. Druse and
William had a good many words. On Thursday before
Christmas, in the morning, William asked me to get up
and build the fire; I did so. Mrs. Druse and Mary then
got up. William went out and did the chores; asked if I
should help; said he would do them himself; when he
came in to breakfast, he sat down to the table; I was
nearly through; Mrs. Druse told me to hurry up; I did so;
I asked her what she wanted; she told me and George to
go out doors and not go far from the house; heard a noise
three or four times, and then she came and called me;
she had a revolver, and she handed it to me and told me
to shoot William or she would shoot me; she put the
revolver against my nose as she told me this; I did so; he
was sitting in a chair or on the floor; I was excited, could
not tell which, and then she took the revolver and shot
until the loads were all out; then she took the ax and
pounded William on the head; William said, "Oh, Roxy,
don't!" Then she chopped his head off, and sent me and
George up stairs after a straw tick; she dragged him on
to it, and she told me I should help drag him in the
parlor, and she asked me to come in there; I told her I
couldn't; then she sent me and George down to the brush
lot after the sharp ax; we came back, she took it in the
other room and shut the door; told me and George to go
up stairs, then she called us down again, and sent us after
some shingles to the hog pen; she built up a hot fire in
both stoves, then had me look out the north window, and
Mary out of south window; then she took a block in
the parlor and a board and chopped him up, as I suppose
she did, and put him in the fire. Then afterwards told me
to put some shingles in the kitchen stove. I saw a large
bone, and the next day she took the ashes up and put
them into a tin spit box which Rudolph Van Evra had

used, and put some of the ashes in a bag; then she told
me to hitch up the horse, as she was going to Mr. Gates;
we all went. When we got into Mr. Ball's swamp, about
two rods from the track, she told me to carry the ashes; I
did so, then went to my house, taken sick and stayed
there until Sunday, when I came back. Mrs. Druse told
me to get the new ax and saw the handle off; I did so,
and Mary burned the handle; then I went to Richfield
Springs with Mrs. Druse; when we got back to
Weatherbee's mill pond, she threw the ax in; when we
got up a little farther, she told me to take the revolver
and throw it into the pond; also the jack knife, or I would
be sorry if I didn't; she threw the razor blade side of the
fence. I did throw the revolver and knife in the pond.
Last night I went with Mr. Filkins, district attorney,
Clarence Marshal and Daniel McDonald to Ball's swamp
where I left the ashes; I showed the ashes to the men;
they put them in a box and brought them to Mr. Pett's ; I
saw the box on table to-day in this room; I went again
to-day with Marshall, McDonald and two strangers, said
to be Doctors; they got all the ashes we could not find
last night; I then went to the pond and showed them as
near as I could where the revolver was, then came home;
the revolver was found in the pond; I did not see the
revolver only as Mr. Marshall put it in his pocket; there
was a newspaper around them when it was thrown into
the pond; I saw it when it went in; I would know the axe;
it was a new ax with small nicks in it, when I brought it
from the woods; sawed the handle off next to the ax,
about an inch from the ax; the handle was wedged in;
think he bought the ax at Richfield Springs; think Druse
put the wedge in at Mr. Pett's; don't know what paper
was around the ax; examining the ax, I think that is
Druse's ax.

District attorney-What makes you think so?

" Because it looks like the ax I sawed the handle off
from. All axes do not look alike. I know this ax by the

nicks in the blade, and the handle being sawed off. Think the ax had no rust or stains on it when I brought it; it has spots on it now."

Was shown a revolver; "That is the one, sir; I know the revolver by the stamped handle and cylinder. The revolver was loaded when thrown into the pond; don't know who loaded it; I know it was loaded, because I saw it. Mrs. Druse told me she got the revolver last fall; she did not say what she got it for."

When I went out of the room at the time Mrs. Druse called me back I left in the room Mrs. Druse, Mary and William; he was eating his breakfast when I went back; his back was towards the outside door. No one else had been there that morning that I know of. Mary was in the kitchen, walking backward and forward between the buttery and parlor door. When I came back in the house, I noticed blood on the back of William's neck, and on the floor; I saw the blood before I fired the revolver. When Mrs. Druse called me, I think he was sitting in the chair, his head was leaning over; I think Mary had the rope around his neck when I came in and was holding him; when I shot the revolver off William made no noise.

By district attorney--Supposing Mr. Pett to be William, show us how you pointed the revolver? Witness points at Mr. Pett with left hand. District attorney-Were you frightened? Ans. "I was when I shot the revolver off; don't know what Mary was doing; Mrs. Druse was behind me; she talked fast when she told me to shoot; but not much faster than usual. George was in the door,;I think. After I shot the revolver off; Mrs. Druse took it.

When I went out of the house I did not know they were going to kill Druse. I did not know what to think when she told me to go out and not go far away. When Mrs.

Druse took the revolver I don't know how many times she shot him; she shot him after I did; I think it hit him.

District attorney-What makes you think she hit him? "Because I could find no holes in the floor or wall."

District attorney-O, then you must have hit him? "Yes sir."

" Did you look to see ? "

" Yes, I looked in the wall."

" What made you do that?"

" Because I wanted to know if he was hit."

Druse fell on the floor; I did not see him fall, I saw him afterwards; his head was near the stove leg; he fell over to the left, his face was towards the stove leg; I saw the top of his head from where I stood. She cut his head off before I went after the sharp ax; she cut it off with an old ax. She said she put his head in the stove first. I don't know where Mary was when she cut the head off; George was up stairs; George did not cry; Mary did on the start. Don't know where the rope came from; I think it was used as a clothesline; Mrs. Druse said she burned the rope up; she said she burned up his vest, inside coat, black overcoat; hat, pants and boots. The bone I saw was in the kitchen stove; it measured about three inches thick, and about fourteen inches long; Mary had the bone; there was some flesh on the ends. I heard them cutting in the parlor; Mrs. Druse was there alone. There were brass buttons on the under coat. Mrs. Druse said she saw Mr. Filkins pass; there were newspapers at the windows. I have only heard Jerry Eckler testify. No one has told me what any one else has sworn to to-day. My father told me William Elwood came to the house and rapped; no one answered. They did not want any one to come in and see what they were doing (evidently not). They were cleaning up the floor. They had big fires to burn Druse up. They had the big boiler on the stove to heat water; I don't know who filled the boiler, think Mrs. Druse did. I saw water only in the boiler, nothing else. They did not boil any part of the body that I know of. I smelled a bad smell, like meat burning.

Mrs. Druse quarreled that morning. I heard Bill say there would be some arrangements made before night. Mary talked low to her mother; Mrs. Druse blowed too; I could hear what they said; I don't know what Mrs. Druse wanted to get rid of Bill for; I heard her say once, " I wish he was gone, because he's so ugly." He was ugly sometimes; she was ugly too; sometimes. I heard them blow each other at times--I mean scold. They did not sleep together; she said she had not slept with him in ten years. Rudolph Van Evera has also slept there; he slept in the farther room up stairs, and they in the front room. George and I slept together. Mary slept with her mother. Never saw Van Evera carry Mrs. Druse up stairs, nor Mary either; don't know of their being up stairs together. My uncle was here from New York one night. My mother and Mrs. Druse are sisters. The knife handle Mrs. Druse burned; Mrs. Druse knew they would know it was his knife; there was blood on it, but she washed it off; she burned up the razor handle; I think it was all right before; don't know why she burned it; she had no saw, she cut him up with the ax, jack-knife and razor. I think I saw blood on her hands; she washed her hands in the kitchen, and then threw the water in the swill pail. The hogs fed themselves that day, in the barn. I could not see the barn from the window I watched at; Mary could from her window. My father came there that night at dark, or a little after; Mrs. Druse let him in; I was there, don't know where he came from; he came in at front door, that opens into the kitchen; the door was not locked, it had been locked nearly all day; father rapped, Mrs. Druse went to the door, she told him to come in; he most always rapped when he came; he sat down and asked for William, if he was at home; she said that he had gone to Mose Elwood's. Father said Will Elwood was down there to-day and rapped but could not get in. He (Elwood) said that he thought Bill had killed them all, and locked himself in, or ran away. My sister said I was not at school, and father came to see where I was. I did not tell him what had happened; I was afraid of Mrs. Druse; she said the first one that told would get shot, and that was the reason I did not tell father. Father was not in the parlor that night; the boiler had been put away; no paint had been put on the floor; water was got from the cistern; I drew it at Mrs. Druse's request; that was after I got the ax.

I told Mr. Pett that William had gone to New York; I told Mr. Filkins also-Mrs. Druse told me to; I told them he went on Sunday. Mary and Mrs. Druse had not breakfasted when Bill was killed; the revolver was not shot off after I came back with the ax; did not know father's revolver was there that day, he had one; Mrs. Druse did not want me to go home; my brother said his orders were to get me; he said some men at Mr. Pett's wanted to see me; Mrs. Druse did not hear this, she had the door locked I think. William had a model of a steamer, which they burned up; they burned it so no one would find it; they said he took it to New York with him.

Last summer they asked me to shoot William, but I saw no revolver; they did not tell where the revolver was bought; I don't know whether the carpet on the parlor floor was taken up or not; I saw no blood on the carpet; carried the ashes away next day; a new piece of oilcloth has been put in the parlor. I was at Jerry Eckler's the day of the murder, to buy a bunch of matches to make the fire with; I got them; I went over after Mr. Filkins and Elwood was there; Mr. Eekler did not ask me about the smell; I gave the matches to Mrs. Druse; Mr. Eakler would take no pay for them. I went to Mr. Pett's too, before that, for matches; there was no one at home; Irving Eckler came there on the morning of the murder for an augur; he did not get it; Mr. Druse said it was over to Mr. Eckler's. Never told of the matter, was afraid Mrs. Druse would shoot me; no other reason. The room casing and wood work in the room have been painted, and the side walls papered, since the murder, and paint put on the floor to hide the blood stains. There had been no talk of painting before. Father noticed the smell and asked me what it was; I told him nothing. We had two lights that night; they were not bright lights. They got the paint in Richfield Springs and the paper at Little Lakes.

William Elwood

Knew Druse, knew he was missing; called at the Druse house on that Thursday; could not get in; windows covered with newspapers; noticed heavy smoke. I saw Filkins about twenty rods from the house; I saw Charles Gates and told him that I had called at Druse's, and that either Bill had killed them all, or they were all dead asleep. The rest of his testimony corroborates earlier statements.

George William Stewart Druse

The nature of an oath, was explained to him, by the district attorney. He said he was ten years of age. George described his various relatives and then told the story of the murder as follows: On the morning when the pistol was used, Frank and I went to the corner of the house; Ma told us to go out; Pa was sitting at the table eating his breakfast; Pa did not hear Ma tell us to go out, because she whispered; Ma had a revolver in her hand; there was no one in the house only Ma, Mary, Pa and Frank; don't know where Uncle Charley was, did not see him; we went out; I heard the revolver go off; Ma called Frank in; when the revolver went off I knew what was being done; Ma said she would hurt Pa; Uncle Charley bought the revolver for her; Frank went in and Ma handed the revolver to him and told Frank to shoot Pa or she would shoot him; Frank shot three times. There was a rope around Pa's neck, and blood on the floor; don't know what Mary was doing, think she was in the kitchen; Ma hit Pa on the head with an ax; he said, "oh, don't."

The rest of George Druse's testimony is nearly the same as Frank's, and corroborates his evidence in nearly all particulars.

Elisha W. Stannard, Wm. R. Wall, Dr. A. D. Getman, Dr. W. P. Booland, Albert Bowen and Chester Crim were sworn, and their testimony taken down by the clerk.

Mrs. Roxy Druse was called to the stand. She said that she did not wish to make any statements, but declared afterward that Chas. Gates was present when her husband died.

James Miller, Chas. Gates, James Hall, Walter Buckman, Geo. L. Rathbun, Mrs. Lucy Gates, Mrs. Elfeha M. Rathbnrn, Cheater Gates, Mrs. Louise Elwood, Moses Elwood, Idella Gates, Irving Eckler, Wm. Elwood, Albert Bowen, Henry Ostrander, Alonzo Filkins, Moses Elwood, Rudolph Vanevry, Frank Gates, Chas. O'Brien; Daniel McDonald, Chas. Bond, and Charles Gates were the other witnesses examined. Their testimony appears in the Coroner's inquest in the order named.

The verdict of the jury was as follows: " That Wm. Druse came to his death on the 18th day of December, 1884, at the town of Warren, and that one Roxana Druse did on the 18th day of December, 1884, between the hours of seven and eleven o'clock of the forenoon of that day, in the town of Warren, in said county, feloniously and of malice aforethought made an assault upon the body of William Druse then and there present, that the said Roxana Druse did shoot William Druse, and also strike him on the head with an ax, and did sever his head from his body; of which wounds the said William Druse died ; that Roxana Druse did cut and burn the body in the stove, and the jurors aforesaid say that the said Roxana Druse did murder her husband. That Mary Druse the daughter, George Druse the son, and Frank Gates were present, and that Frank Gates did fire one or more shots at William Druse, and that Mary, George and Frank did comfort, aid and abet Roxana Druse in committing the felony and murder."

At the conclusion of the inquest sheriff Valentine Brown, who was present during the entire proceedings before the coroner, placed his four prisoners in a close-covered sleigh and drove rapidly over the snowy hills for the county seat. The sheriff left Little Lakes about half-past three o'clock on Wednesday afternoon, arriving at the Herkimer jail about seven in the evening. During the trip the murderess evinced a remarkable degree of nerve, and appeared to be totally unconcerned over the situation of affairs. She remarked that "whether it turned out state prison for life, or hanging, she would never live with Wm. Druse again," meaning probably, that she would prefer either, rather than live with her dead husband. Undoubtedly the wish so coolly uttered, will be granted. The other prisoners exhibited no care, the two boys especially, amusing themselves by making jovial comments on objects that elicited their interest along the road.

On arriving at the jail they were met by a curious crowd, but were hurried at once to the general waiting room. After a few moments rest, they were informed that their quarters were ready, and as Mrs. Druse arose to accompany the jailer she remarked in an offhand manner: "Well, I hope I may be able to procure to-night what I have not had before in two years, a good night's rest." The two women were placed in a warm and comfortable room in the upper portion of the building, and the two boys on the upper tier, in the general quarters assigned to the prisoners.

A day or two after the arrival of the prisoners, the writer visited the jail at Herkimer, and accompanied by Henry Brown, was shown to the room of Mrs. Druse and Mary. On entering, we found the mother and daughter seated near the heavily barred window, engaged in close conversation, which was interrupted as we crossed the threshold. After the usual preliminary introduction, we seated ourselves and at once plunged into the object of our visit. Throughout our conversation with her mother, Mary kept her eyes bent on the floor, only raising them at intervals to watch her mother's face. She said nothing during the interview. We asked her if Charles Gates was present when the deed was committed. She replied that he was. In response to a question in relation to Charles Gates' knowledge of the disposition of the body, she said that he knew more about that than any one else, as he was present and afterwards assisted in disposing of the remains. She also stated that in .her opinion Chas. Gates should have been held, as by so doing certain things would have been brought out that could not be gained, otherwise. She was firm in her statement that Gates was present, and reiterated the remark two or three times over. She appeared cool and unconcerned, and it was evident to the most casual observer that very little love existed between herself and husband. She appeared to consider that in ridding the world of William Druse, she had performed an action that was in the highest degree commendable, and that all right minded persons would sympathize with her as the victim of circumstances and not as a heartless and cold-blooded murderess.

After leaving the cell of this female fiend, we turned down stairs, and amid the clanging of innumerable bolts and bars, and the clicking of locks, found ourselves on the south tier in the ground department. From the midst of the throng of prisoners our conductor picked out the two boys, and we called them toward us for a talk. George Druse is about ten years of age, is short in stature, round, full form, and at the time of our visit was clad in a blue cloth suit and rubber boots. He had a round, full face, indicative of fun and good nature, and taken altogether appeared as a bright, intelligent boy, who little realized the terrible curse which had fallen on the family. He did not have much to say in relation to the affair, the sum of his remarks being about the same as already presented heretofore.

Frank Gates was questioned closely in regard to his connection with the crime. We asked him if his father, Charles Gates, was present when the murder was committed. He replied emphatically, " No." We asked him at what time his father visited the house, he said, "the same evening," and also stated that his father did not learn of the murder of Druse when he called. Frank also said that Mrs. Druse had "scared the life out of him," that he was afraid that she would kill him if he did not do as she ordered; that during the time that Mrs. Druse was cutting up the body she repeatedly threatened to kill him if he breathed a word in relation to the murder.

He said that the terrible scene made him so deathly sick to his stomach that he was forced to go outdoors, where he fainted dead away from fright and horror.

On the 29th day of January the Druses were brought before Judge T. C. Murray, when they waived examination, and were again remanded to jail.
Judge Amos A. Prescott of Herkimer, for sixteen years county judge of this county; has been retained by attorney Luce, of Richfield Springs, as associate counsel in the case.

Considerable excitement was manifested on or about March 20th, by the reported finding of the missing head of Wm Druse, in a sap bush located in the town of Warren. The rumor, on investigation, proved to be without foundation. But as suspicious circumstances tended to prove that something had been hidden in the sap house, and then removed, constables Sylvester Wilson and Joseph W. Smith, of Herkimer, visited the place, and on a warrant sworn out before Judge Helmer by district attorney Steels, arrested William Elwood. Elwood protested his innocence, but was brought to Herkimer and placed in jail. During his incarceration Elwood's friends succeeded in securing the services of Judge George W. Smith and J. A. Steele as counsel: :Elwood was finally brought before Judge Wm. Helmer, and after a short examination was released on bail of $2,000.

The Middleville Tragedy, 1885

Professor S. Clark Smith, of Fairfield, Shot through the Heart by Dr. Moritz R. Richter of Middleville.
Family Troubles at the Bottom of the Affair

There is an old French saying, to the effect, "That one murder or suicide in a locality is sure to be followed by another." Herkimer county has given us a realizing sense of its truth, as the foul demon of murder has run riot over its fair surface during the past year.

Following rapidly on the heels of the Druse butchery comes the Middleville tragedy. The people of the county were still engaged in using the Druse affair as a subject of conversation when they were startled to learn that another capital crime had been added to the already long list. The particulars of this murder are still fresh in the minds of the people, and are substantially as follows:

On the 28th day of last February, Dr. Moritz R. Richter, a German physician, resident of the village of Middleville; shot and killed Professor S. Clark Smith, of Fairfield. At five o'clock, coroner I. O. Nellis, of Herkimer, received a telephone despatch from Middleville, summoning him to that place at once, as a murder had been committed in the village. The despatch also called for the attendance of district attorney A. B. Steele, but as that official was ill and unable to go, he sent his law partner, William C: Prescott. Coroner Nellis, William C. Prescott, and A. T. Smith, the Utica Herald representative, drove to the scene of the tragedy, and on arrival found the town wild with excitement. Coroner Dr. A. J. Browns, of Newport, was on the ground and had already impanneled a jury. The prisoner was under arrest, in charge of deputy sheriff De Witt Jerkins and constable Taber.

The Doctor's statement of the facts leading up to the affair, is as follows:

Dr. Richter was born in the city of Bischoffswerter, Kingdom of Saxony, November 17th, 1825, and will be 60 years old next November. He studied medicine and graduated from the University of Leipsic. Richter came to this country in 1854, and located at Middleville, where he has since resided. He was naturalized September 13th, 1859, and for 15 or 20 years had a large and lucrative practice in the northern part of the county. He was a skillful physician, and many of his patients had implicit confidence in his knowledge. He owned a small place, one and. one-third acres,-in the village, with a story and a half house, and a small office attached. The office was not kept open in the winter; the doctor treating his patients in the house.

Until 1876 he lived alone, taking his meals with a neighbor, Mrs. Laura Harter by name. In the above year he married Miss Eliza Ward, a daughter of the late Sidney D. Ward, who formerly resided on a farm in the town of Little Falls. The marriage took place without the consent or knowledge of Miss Ward's parents. When her father was informed of it, he was much surprised, and exclaimed, "that he would as soon thought of being struck on the head with an ax as to hear of his daughter's marriage with Richter."

The doctor and his wife lived happily together until about a year ago, then, according the doctor's statement, after returning home from a few days absence, his wife acted strangely. One of the pupils of her eye was enlarged and from this he thought her partially insane. In February, 1884, he took her to her father's home, where she has since resided. She left with the doctor her clothing, jewelry, furs, etc.

S. Clark Smith came to Middleville on the 28th.of February, with a bill of sale signed by Mrs. Richter, for $200, selling to Smith all her personal property. Smith applied to Dr. Hamlin, Justice of the Peace, for relevant papers, but not obtaining them went to Newport where the papers were procured

In company with Mr. Getman, his brother-in-law, Smith went to Richter's residence at 11 A.M. The Doctor's statement of what then took place is as follows: .

"Smith came in with his brother-in-law; I was glad to see them and asked them to take a chair; Smith replied that he had come after my wife's clothing, and showed me a bill of sale;. I said; I will tell you what I will do, Clark; I will send her trunk, in which are her clothes, rings and jewelry, her valuable mink furs, shoes and other articles of clothing, if you will take them and be satisfied, until I can see my wife; or if, she refuses to see me, until I can consult counsel. He said, very well, I suppose I shall have to. We went up stairs, and I tied up the boxes and he and I carried down the trunk, setting it in the front door, and from there it was taken out and put in the sleigh.

A short time after a patient called, and while he was there Smith and Getman came back again, and Smith wanted to know if I would give up my wife's mortgage, which she held on the plaice., (Mrs. Richter held two mortgages on the place, amounting to $725) I said, wait until I see my wife and have counsel. He went away, but came the third time, between four and five p. m., in company with constable Charles Taber and his brother, John Taber. I explained matters to the constable, and told Clark that I considered my wife partially insane, and not competent to transact business, and said, if you take anything else away, you do it at the risk of your lives. They showed me the bill of sale for $200. The goods were worth at least $600."

Smith and officer Taber went upstairs and were followed by the Doctor. John Taber remained below. Smith pointed out a chamber set, which the officer was to take, and while standing with his back to the physician, Richter shot him in the back. Taber quickly turned, when the doctor followed with another shot, Smith having partially turned the ball entered under the left arm. Smith staggered toward the head of the stairs, exclaimed "My God, I'm shot!" ran down stairs, staggered across the yard—a distance of twenty-five feet--and fell dead in the snow.

Officer Taber, as soon as he heard the shot, advanced toward Richter, who, he says, pointed the pistol at him. He grasped him, but the doctor was the stronger of the two, and threw Taber on the bed. He called for help; John Taber came in, grasped Richter around the body, and wrenched the pistol from his hand. Richter was at once handcuffed and taken to Doctor Hamlin's office. The pistol with which the shooting was done is a small four-shooter, of the Elliott make, ring lock, carrying a 38 calibre ball. When taken from the doctor it had in it two empty and two loaded cartridges.

The post mortem examination, held by Dr. C. W. Hamlin, assisted by Coroner Nellis, of Herkimer, revealed the course of the bullets. The first shot entered through the fifth intercostal space, a short distance to the right of the spine. It was found in front, just under the skin, nearly opposite the place of entrance, and near the medium line of the sternum on the right. The bullet was found to have shattered the fifth rib, carrying fragments of bone into the right lung, and thence passing onward through the lung and interior walls of the chest to the skin. This wound alone would have caused death.

The second bullet entered the left chest on its outer and anterior aspect, and passing into the chest through the third intercostal space, carried fragments of the bone into the left lung. The bullet then deflected downward, passing through the left lung, through the posterior part of the left auricle of the heart, and then through the right ventricle. The track of the bullet, as it emerged froth the heart, was nearly on the same plane as the other shot as it passed through the chest. The tissues at that point were very much lacerated. No point where the bullet left the body could be found. The chest was filled with blood on both sides, and apparently all the blood in the system had escaped into the plural sac. Both lungs were completely collapsed. This wound also would have caused death. Smith, after receiving his wounds, had gone eighty-two feet before he fell. (This is a point for the doctors, and can be considered remarkable, as the man was shot through the heart.)

The Coroner's inquest was adjourned until the next day, and the prisoner in the mean time taken to the county jail at Herkimer, by officer Taber and Dewitt Jenkins, deputy sheriff. Middleville the next morning was crowded with teams, hundreds of people from the surrounding towns gathering around Parkhurst hall, where the inquest was held. The Doctor's abilities as a physician were abundantly recognized, and the qualities of the principals in the case freely commented upon. The fact that the Doctor had been educated in Germany, was a sufficient guarantee of his ability, and he had accordingly worked up a large practice, which in late years he had largely lost, mostly on account of his eccentricities. He. was very fond of playing cards, checkers and chess, and when in the middle of a game would refuse to leave, no matter how urgent the call. In consequence he was considered unreliable, and his clients fell away from him. His life became embittered, and together with his domestic troubles culminated finally in the tragedy.

The witnesses examined before the Coroner were Melvin Getman, Charles W. Taber, John Taber, Dr. C. W. Hamlin and Dr. I. O. Nellis. The sum and substance of the testimony is already embraced in the foregoing account.

After hearing the evidence, the jury retired, and shortly afterwards brought in the following verdict: "That S.

Clark Smith came to his death from wounds received from a pistol or revolver in the hands of Moritz R. Richter, inflicted by him with the premeditated design of effecting the death of said S. Clark Smith, and that said killing, in the opinion of the jury, was murder in the first degree."

District attorney A. B. Steele was present during the inquest, and assisted the coroner in the examination of witnesses. Since the inquest Dr. Richter has secured the legal services of Judge George W. Smith and J. A. Steele, of Herkimer. The property owned by Richter has been sold at auction; that portion claimed by the wife being placed in her possession. The funeral of the murdered man took place at the Universalist church, Herkimer, March 4th, the Rev. Dr. G. W. Powell officiating.

Dr. Richter, a day or two after his arrival in Herkimer, made the following statement:

That much of the trouble has been brought about by his wife's relatives, and that scheming on their part brought on his wife's insanity. He claimed that he never had any difficulty with his wife, and that she has uniformly expressed her good will toward him, and that he never had said an unkind word to her. He last saw her last July at the time of the Huyck shooting at Eatonville. Her people would not allow him to visit her. He said that people at Middleville have sought to ruin his practice, and that he is isolated and alone in the world, and that his prosperity is blasted. He seemed to be in the depth of despair--no wife, his house mortgaged for all it was worth, and, by the bill of sale held by Smith. Even that would have been stripped of everything within it that would make it comfortable. Referring to Smith, he declared that he did not like him, that he was obnoxious and disagreeable, that when he carne to his house in the

afternoon it made him frantic. He was very sorry that he
had shot any one, but--what could he do ? When asked if
it was so that he attempted to shoot officer Taber, he
replied, " No, indeed, if I had shot any one it would have
been myself."

There is no question but what the murder was
premeditated, but owing to the many circumstances
connected with the sorrowful affair, I do not deem
it advisable to publish comments. Let the law take its
course.

"Conversation of the Skulls"

At the conclusion of his description of the murder of William Eacker, W.H. Tippett included the following "Conversation of the Skulls," adding this explanation:

-editor

The introduction of the skulls as evidence, so affected one of the jurymen that he evolved the following unique specimen of ghastly literature. The article in question was handed to me by district attorney Steele, and I here present it for the edification of the reader:

-W.H.T.

Scene 1st.--Herkimer County Court House, Court in Session and Full House.

Why am I here in this ill-ventilated room? Let me listen a moment and I soon shall learn, meanwhile I will observe the crowd.

This young man who sits near me has a very good-natured and pleasant countenance, so I think he is not dangerous, though there is no person who bears a harder name, or whose temper is more frequently spoken of, than his.

The next one near me has a name suggestive of labor and manufacturing, and ought therefore to be a productive and useful member of society.

Who is this just below me? A small, quick, nervous man,--yet he speaks well and will probably leave no stone unturned that he deems will be of help to him. He seems to be associated with one of a tall and commanding appearance, whose movements and words indicate moderation and caution, whose language and gestures are impressive, and when he speaks the audience is hushed.

Little thinks this active man, as he takes me from hand to hand with careless gestures, that the ethereal essence - the invisible spirit - has for the time returned to its former habitation; that the blank cavities, where once rolled the sparkling orbs, are even now filled with the spiritual eyes,--now looking out at him and upon all before me.

Each sound now vibrates on the spiritual ear, and the essence of the brain that once filled this dome is present, conscious and active.

These frightful sockets were once filled with eyes as dark as night, whose languishing looks of love melted many a youthful heart, whose sparkling flashes of wit or smiles of pleasure charmed and enlivened my friends, and whose glances of anger or of scorn silenced or abashed my foes.

Long is the time since this bare bone was crowned with beautiful flowing ringlets (and all my own), that were praised by my admirers or envied by my rivals.

But these memories crowding around me are needless here; to all this assembly I am only a grinning, hideous skull, suggestive of death, decay and dust. People look on me with averted eyes, as a horrible sight; unpleasant thoughts arise in their minds, and they believe the sexton has failed in his duty.

Some of these heads now before me may in after years grin in a doctor's office, or grace (!) the museum of some phrenologist--(I think that is the word, though I have but lately heard it),--or perhaps be brought out on some public occasion like this to add terror to the language of a learned doctor of law. Only hear him now, as he irreverently takes the wrappings from me, and holds me up to the gaze of the court and jury. How flippantly he speaks; he tells of "frontal bones" and "occepital," of "temporal bones" and "dusa mater," of "arteries and veins," of "fractures," "hemorrhages" and "congestions."

With patience must I bear these uses and comfort myself with the thought that, sooner or later, other empty skulls may come to court.

The shades of evening are falling; the business of the day is drawing to a close with earthly things; to me no day, no night is known.

Spirits belong to eternity, and while these drowsy mortals pass a space of time in sleep I will visit other scenes, to reappear again on what is called to-morrow.

While all are wrapt in silent slumber I. will hover near them, holding converse with their spirits in the language of dreams, though the unconscious body lies in the counterfeit of death.

The coming morn you may hear these persons tell of dreaming of dead or absent friends, of skeletons and skulls, or of kicks, congestions, drunkenness and death.

Scene 2d.--Scene, The Court House.

lst Skull, Solus:

Again I am brought out and exposed to all the rabble, I almost said alone, but there is another skull near me--a more aged one; this is better, to be alone is not well. I will address the stranger. Who art thou and (enter 2d Skull) why art thou here?

2d Skull:

My name may not be spoken; I am here to gratify the common desire of human beings to not be excelled by their rivals; if your friends can afford to have a skull so can mine.

But with spirits there should be no rivalry; we will speak of the scene now before us.

How many years of human counting have rolled away since you left the flesh?

1st Skull:

Full half a century has departed since these bones were clothed in beauty,--since thoughts of love, hopes of honor and the pride of youth were suddenly cut off by relentless Death, and my immortal soul was set free from the fetters of flesh and has since ranged the boundless eternity.

2d Skull:

But why is this gathering and this war of words:

1st Skull:

Listen and you will learn,--the old story of wrong that is ever rehearsing by men on earth. In the flesh you probably knew and realized something of the enemy that men take to steal their brains away. Anger and revenge have been at work, and death and sorrow have resulted; here are fragments of a skull broken in a fray, and the offender in now waiting for the punishment soon to be measured to him.

2d Skull:

I see; but my bones would have borne a heavier blow--
my skull is thick. Things are different in this age; time
works great changes. When I was in the old jail here,
seventy years ago, heads bore more bruising than now.

1st Skull:

Let us speak of other things. I hardly understand how I
was brought here so rapidly; truly spirits know no time
or space, yet our did homes must be carried about--they
are matter.

2d Skull:

Have you not heard of the great discoveries of mortals
spiritualizing water. With great heat they drive off the
grosser parts, and then the loosened spirit becomes a
mighty power. Mortals confine it and make it do the
work of countless horses. It propels large ships across
the ocean, turns the wheels of vast manufactories, and
moves men and merchandise with wonderful speed.

1st Skull:

Again I ask,--my curiosity is excited. Yestermorn I was
quietly reposing in a dark closet; my owner was here; he
wanted me; he sent for me in an instant of time. How is
this done -- send with the rapidity of thought?

2d Skull:

Man has tamed the lightning, turned it to his own use,
and with it flashes his thoughts around the world.

1st Skull:

I will speak of more congenial subjects,--as our time is short here I wish to improve it. I see by the females here that they are still the slaves of fashion, as I fear they ever will be. My attention is very naturally directed to the head, and I observe that the bonnets are so small, but they are so by reason of the unnatural form of the heads of this age. The unsightly and large excresence on the back of the head makes it impossible to put a comfortable bonnet upon it. I have understood that this was formed artificially at first, but as this imposed much hard labor on the wearer, the heads of the weaker sex are now formed with this protuberance by nature. This will be likely to cause a new departure in what these moderns call phrenology, but I do not doubt but these learned men will be equal to the emergency, as there is no increase of brains in these new heads, but rather the contrary.

2d Skull:

I hear you have not lost your old habit of much talking, and that curiosity is still a virtue with your sex. But our conversation must cease, as our friends seem to be leaving, and besides for some time I have observed one who appeared to be listening to us,--and possibly he has heard all we have said.

1st Skull:

 You are like all the men, ever accusing us of much talking; and if one did hear us I hope he will hear that I have had the last word.

Herkimer County Officials
from 1791 to 1885

COUNTY JUDGES.--Ezra Graves, June, 1847,
November, 1859; Robert Earl, 1855; Volney Owen,
1863; Amos H. Prescott, 1867; Rollin H.
Smith, 1883.

COUNTY CLERKS.--Jonas Platt, February 17, 1791 ;
Joab Griswold, March 19, 1798; Elilhu Griswold, April
6, 1804, and March 4, 1811; Peter
M. Myers, February 28, 1810, and February 23, 1813;
Aaron Hackley, Jr., February 12, 1812, and February 16,
1815; Walter Fish, April 16, 1817;
John Mahon, February 13, 1821; Jabez Fox, 1822;
Abijah Beckwith, 1825; Julius C. Nelson, 1831; John
Dygert, 1834; Erwin A. Munson, 1840;
Standish Barry, 1846; Elkanah T. Cleland, 1852 ;
Cornelius T. E. Van Horne, 1855; Zenas Greene, 1861;
Douglass Bennett, 1867 and 1870: Edward
Simms, 1873 and 1876; P. M. Wood, 1879 and 1882.

SHERIFFS.--William Colbraith, February 17, 1791, and
February 9, 1796; Peter Smith, February 18, 1795;
Chauncey Woodruff, March 19,
1798; William H. Cook, March 17, 1802, and March 5,
1807; Ephriam Snow, March 6, 1806; John Mahon,
February 22, 1808, March 4, 1811, and
March 2, 1815; Philo M. Hackley, February 28, 1810;
Henry Hopkins, February 23, 1813; Robert Shoemaker,
February 13, 1817; Stephen Hallett,
February 13, 1821, and November, 1822; John Dygert,
1825; John Graves, 1828; Frederick P. Bellinger, 1831;
Francis E. Spinner, 1834; Stephen W.
Brown, 1837; William C. Crain, 1840; Jeremiah Corey,
1843; William I. Skinner, 1846; Daniel Hawn. 1849;
Lorenzo Carryl, 1852; Peter

Countryman, 1855; James J. Cook, 1858; Seth M. Richmond, 1861; George M. Cleland, 1864; James H. Weatherwax, 1867; Alexander Smith, 1870; Volney Eaton, 1873; James H. Ives, 1876; D. C. Paine, 1879; Valentine Brown, 1882.

DISTRICT ATTORNEYS --Thomas R. Gold, February 26, 1797; Nathan Williams, August 20, 1801; Joseph Kirkland, February 23, 1813; Thomas H. Hubbard, February 26, 1816; Simeon Ford, June 11, 1818, and September, 1836; Michael Hoffman, May, 1823 and March, 1836; George H. Feeter, 1825; Aaron Hackley, 1828; James B. Hunt, 1833; Dudley Burwell, 1836; Hiram Nolton, 1837; George B. Judd, June, 1847; Volney Owen, 1850; Lauren Ford, 1856; George A. Hardin, January 28, 1858, and elected in the following November; Clinton A. Moon, 1861; Sewell S. Morgan, 1864; Charles G. Burrows, 1867; Albert M. Mills, 1870 and 1873; J. J. Dudleston, Jr., 1876; Abram B. Steele, 1879 and 1882.

COUNTY TREASURERS.*-Robert Ethridge, 1848 and 1866; Horatio N. Johnson, 1851; C. C. Witherstine, 1854; Allen W. Eaton, 1857; Floyd C. Shepard, 1863; Alphonso D. Marshall, 1872; Albert Story, 1878; Caleb P. Miller, 1884.

*County Treasurers were appointed by Boards of Supervisors before 1846, and held office for three years.

This book is available at:

http://stores.lulu.com/ wilderness hill

Wilderness Hill Books
75 Wilderness Lane
Valatie, New York 12184

wildernesshill@ gmail.com

Printed in the United States
145981LV00001B/66/P